"Don't you *need to trust* me?"*

Mark looked at her for a long moment.

"I don't understand what you mean."

"You're going to be coming to my home, plus you said we'd be going on outings with Joey. We'll also have private meetings such as this one to discuss progress. I'm referring to you trusting me as a man, not just as Joey's guardian. Do you trust me as a man?"

"I…" Cedar stopped speaking.

Why was Mark doing this? She didn't intend to view him as a *man*. No, he was Joey's guardian, his uncle, the person who was now that little boy's father. Their relationship had nothing to do with Cedar, the woman, trusting Mark, the man.

Mark Chandler unsettled her, made her acutely aware of her femininity and his incredible masculinity. She had no idea if she trusted him.

She was having enough trouble trusting *herself* whenever she was near him.

Dear Reader,

Well, it's September, which always sounds like a fresh start to me, no matter how old I get. And evidently we have six women this month who agree. In *Home Again* by Joan Elliott Pickart, a woman who can't have children has decided to work with them in a professional capacity—but when she is assigned an orphaned little boy, she fears she's in over her head. Then she meets his gorgeous guardian—and she's *sure* of it!

In the next installment of MOST LIKELY TO…, *The Measure of a Man* by Marie Ferrarella, a single mother attempting to help her beloved former professor joins forces with a former campus golden boy, now the college…custodian. What could have happened? Allison Leigh's *The Tycoon's Marriage Bid* pits a pregnant secretary against her ex-boss who, unbeknownst to him, has a real connection to her baby's father. In *The Other Side of Paradise* by Laurie Paige, next up in her SEVEN DEVILS miniseries, a mysterious woman seeking refuge as a ranch hand learns that she may have more ties to the community than she could have ever suspected. When a beautiful nurse is assigned to care for a devastatingly handsome, if cantankerous, cowboy, the results are…well, you get the picture—but you can have it spelled out for you in Stella Bagwell's next MEN OF THE WEST book, *Taming a Dark Horse*. And in *Undercover Nanny* by Wendy Warren, a domestically challenged female detective decides it's necessary to penetrate the lair of single father and heir to a grocery fortune by pretending to be…his nanny. Hmm. It *could* work.…

So enjoy, and snuggle up. Fall weather is just around the corner.…

Happy reading!

Gail Chasan
Senior Editor

Please address questions and book requests to:
Silhouette Reader Service
U.S.: 3010 Walden Ave., P.O. Box 1325, Buffalo, NY 14269
Canadian: P.O. Box 609, Fort Erie, Ont. L2A 5X3

JOAN ELLIOTT PICKART

Home Again

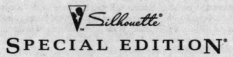

Silhouette

SPECIAL EDITION

Published by Silhouette Books

America's Publisher of Contemporary Romance

For Janet Elliott and Pat Elliott Hunt.
My sisters, my friends.

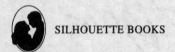 SILHOUETTE BOOKS

ISBN 0-373-24705-2

HOME AGAIN

Visit Silhouette Books at www.eHarlequin.com

Printed in U.S.A.

Books by Joan Elliott Pickart

Silhouette Special Edition

*Friends, Lovers...and
  Babies! #1011
*The Father of Her Child #1025
†Texas Dawn #1100
†Texas Baby #1141
Wife Most Wanted #1160
The Rancher and the Amnesiac Bride #1204
∆The Irresistible Mr. Sinclair #1256
∆The Most Eligible M.D. #1262
Man...Mercenary...Monarch #1303
*To a MacAllister Born #1329
*Her Little Secret #1377
Single with Twins #1405
◊The Royal MacAllister #1477
◊Tall, Dark and Irresistible #1507
◊The Marrying MacAllister #1579
◊Accidental Family #1616
The Homecoming Hero Returns #1694
Home Again #1705

Silhouette Desire

*Angels and Elves #961
Apache Dream Bride #999
†Texas Moon #1051
†Texas Glory #1088
Just My Joe #1202
∆Taming Tall, Dark Brandon #1223
*Baby: MacAllister-Made #1326
*Plain Jane MacAllister #1462

Silhouette Books

*His Secret Son
◊Party of Three
◊Crowned Hearts
  "A Wish and a Prince"

*The Baby Bet
†Family Men
∆The Bachelor Bet
◊The Baby Bet: MacAllister's Gifts

Previously published under the pseudonym Robin Elliott

Silhouette Special Edition

Rancher's Heaven #909
Mother at Heart #968

Silhouette Intimate Moments

Gauntlet Run #206

Silhouette Desire

Call It Love #213
To Have It All #237
Picture of Love #261
Pennies in the Fountain #275
Dawn's Gift #303
Brooke's Chance #323
Betting Man #344
Silver Sands #362
Lost and Found #384
Out of the Cold #440
Sophie's Attic #725
Not Just Another Perfect Wife #818
Haven's Call #859

JOAN ELLIOTT PICKART

is the author of over ninety-five novels. When she isn't writing, she enjoys reading, needlework, gardening and attending craft shows on the town square. Joan has three all-grown-up daughters as well as a young daughter, Autumn, who is in elementary school. Joan, Autumn, and a three-pound poodle named Willow live in a charming small town in the high pine country of Arizona.

Dear Puncho:

I wish I could smile whole bunches like you do 'cause you look happy all the time. I don't feel too happy 'cause my mom and dad went in the car and now they are angels and I miss them whole lots. My uncle Mark is sort of okay when he's not grumpy and Cedar is way cool and I think they would be a good family for me but I don't know if they want to be my family or not. Could you try real hard to make them be my family so I won't be lonely?

Your friend,

Joey

Chapter One

Cedar Kennedy glanced at her watch and frowned. Her new client was ten minutes late for his five-o'clock appointment. Remembering that her secretary had left early for a dreaded trip to the dentist, Cedar picked up the files she'd been updating and walked to the outer office, where she placed the folders in Bethany's in-box.

She sat down in the chair behind the desk and flipped the page in the leather-bound appointment book to see what was on the agenda for tomorrow. Just as she closed the book, the door to the suite opened and a man entered, shoving the door closed behind him.

In one quick perusal Cedar observed that her visitor was tall, with broad shoulders that stretched the material of a faded plaid shirt to the maximum, long legs clad in dusty jeans, and he was wearing heavy work boots. His features…goodness gracious… were rugged and blatantly masculine, his square jaw covered in an obvious five-o'clock shadow. He had thick black hair badly in need of a trim and extremely dark eyes that swept over the reception area before meeting her gaze as he approached the desk.

This was one very earthy, handsome man, Cedar decided. *Very* handsome. And, if she were correct, he was also late for his appointment, and she fully intended to make clear that being on time was of the utmost importance.

"Mr. Chandler?" Cedar asked, getting to her feet.

"Yeah, I'm Mark Chandler," he said.

Perfect voice, Cedar thought. Deep, sort of rumbly, befitting a man of his size and physique.

Mark Chandler glanced at the open door leading to her office and lowered his voice. "I'm a little late for my appointment," he said. "Is this doc a real stickler about people being on time?" He looked at the nameplate on the desk. "I'd hate to start out on the wrong foot, Bethany…you know what I mean?

I'm a desperate man and I need this doc's help. Big-time."

He swiped the front of one thigh, then the other. "How does she feel about construction-site dust? I didn't have a spare second to go home to shower and change clothes."

Cedar snapped her head back up to meet Mark Chandler's gaze. She'd been watching the fascinating motion of his large hand on those mus-cled thighs and…oh, good grief…now he was dragging that hand through his thick hair in a ges-ture so incredibly male it was enough to make a woman weep.

"I…" She stopped to clear her throat when she heard the strange little squeak that used to be her voice.

"I've never talked to a shrink before," Mark con-tinued. "Is she all stuffy? Does she just nod a lot and say 'mmm'? Man, I'm so out of my league being here, but I'm at the end of my rope. What's the best way to get on the good side of this Dr. Kennedy, make her forget I blew it by being late?"

"Mmm," Cedar said, because she couldn't resist, then frowned thoughtfully for good measure. "I per-sonally don't think that Dr. Kennedy is stuffy at all, Mr. Chandler. I'd suggest that you apologize for your tardiness and make it clear that you'll be on time for future appointments."

"Yeah, okay, I can handle that. Well, go for it. Tell the shrinky-dink that I'm here."

"The shrinky-dink?" Cedar said, her eyes widening. "Dr. Kennedy is a psychologist, Mr. Chandler."

"Whatever." Mark sighed. "Man, I'm beat. It was a long, rough day on the job. I'm tired, hungry and need a shower, so let's get this show on the road."

"By all means," Cedar said, rising from the chair. "Heaven forbid that you should be kept waiting now that you've graced us with your presence. Promptness is a virtue, Mr. Chandler. You'd do well to remember that."

"You had a long day, too, huh? I mean, you're not exactly Miss Sunshine, Bethany. You're a very attractive woman, but I bet you'd be even prettier if you smiled."

"Follow me, please," Cedar said, walking past Mark toward her office.

"Anywhere," Mark said, then cringed when the receptionist glared at him over her shoulder.

Nice, Mark thought, his gaze sweeping over Bethany as he trudged slowly behind. She had short, wavy blond hair, delicate features, and sensational blue eyes. Her navy slacks and pale-blue sweater revealed she had curves in all the right places. Oh, yeah, very nice. Except for the fact that she was a tad grumpy.

They entered the doctor's large, comfortably furnished office and Bethany motioned for him to sit in one of the two easy chairs fronting a mahogany desk. Mark sank into one of the chairs and propped the ankle of one leg on the knee of the other.

She stared at him for a long moment, then walked slowly behind the desk to settle into a high-backed leather chair.

"Mr. Chandler," she said, folding her hands atop a file on the desk. "I'm Dr. Cedar Kennedy. Please be on time for your appointments in the future, and if that sounds stuffy, tough."

"Oh-h-h, hell," Mark said, closing his eyes for a moment, before looking at her again. "You're not the receptionist?"

"No."

"You might have said something before I made a total jerk of myself," he said.

"But you were doing such a terrific job of it, I hated to interrupt."

"Okay, okay," Mark said, raising both hands in a gesture of peace. "Could we start over? I'm sorry I was late. It won't happen again. I'm sorry I'm getting your plushy office dusty. That *will* probably happen again. Look, I need your help and Dr. Gibson, my personal doctor, said you're the best in the business for dealing with my kind of problem. Will you help me? Please?"

Cedar sank back into her chair and smiled at Mark Chandler. "I'll certainly try," she said. "Now then, why don't you tell me why you're here. Just let the words flow and I'll take some notes as you speak. That way I can... Is something wrong? You're look-ing at me so...so intently as though I suddenly grew a second nose or something."

"What? Oh, sorry. I didn't realize I was doing that, but...I said earlier you'd be even prettier if you smiled, but that doesn't even begin to cut it. Your face just lit up and your eyes actually sparkled. I've never seen eyes sparkle before. Are you wearing contact lenses?"

"No, I'm not," Cedar said, feeling a warm flush stain her cheeks as she digested Mark's compli-ments.

This will never do, she admonished herself. This rough-hewn hunk was throwing her totally off-kil-ter and that wasn't like her at all, not one little bit. She had to regain control of this situation...right now. She was reacting to Mark on a personal level rather than a professional one, and that would never do.

"Mr. Chandler," she said coolly, "the clock is run-ning and we're wasting valuable time here. Shall we get down to business?"

"You're ticked," he said. "Is there a rule that says

a guy isn't supposed to tell the shrink she's a beautiful woman? Like I said, I've never talked to a shrink—ah, excuse me—a *psychologist* before. Could you give me a little slack on the protocol thing?"

"Agreed," Cedar said. "Now, tell me, why are you here?"

He sighed. It was a defeated-sounding sigh that seemed to come from the very depths of his soul. Cedar leaned forward, encouraging Mark to talk.

"I'm here because of Joey," he said quietly. "He's so damn sad and I can't reach him no matter what I do. He's got walls built around himself and he won't let me get close to him. We can't go on like this."

Cedar opened the file on her desk and wrote Joey on the paper inside.

Who was Joey? she wondered, waiting for Mark to continue. From the pain in his voice it was obvious that Joey was very important to him. Dr. Gibson knew her specialty, so Cedar could hazard one guess as to who Joey was.

"I'm sorry, Mr. Chandler," she said. "I'm afraid I'm at a bit of a disadvantage. If she were here, Bethany would have had you fill out a form as a new client but I failed to do that. Normally, I would know who Joey is by reading that information. I'll remember to give you the form after our session. Right now, why don't we just talk? Are you married? Is Joey your son?"

"No, I'm not married. Never have been. Joey is my nephew."

Hooray, Mark Chandler isn't married, Cedar thought, then swallowed heavily. Where on earth had that reaction come from? Talk about unprofessional. And talk about out of character for her to be so focused on the physical attributes and marital status of a man she'd just met. This was absurd. She was just tired, that's all. It had been a very long, busy day. Fine. She was okay now.

"Your nephew," she repeated, writing the fact on the sheet. "How old is he?"

"Seven."

"Why don't you tell me about Joey?"

Mark sighed again. "He's my sister Mary's son. Mary and her husband, John, were killed in an automobile accident two months ago. Joey wasn't in the car because he was spending the night at a friend's house."

Cedar nodded and made more notes on the paper.

"I flew to New York for the funeral and was there about three weeks taking care of legal matters. Joey spent a lot of time at the neighbor's house during those weeks because I was very busy. Finally, though, I was able to bring him back here to Phoenix. I'm Joey's legal guardian, you see."

"How did he feel about all that?"

Mark shrugged. "He didn't really react at all. He's like a zombie. He hardly talks to me, spends most of his time alone in his bedroom, and just seems to be operating in his own little world where no one is allowed to enter. I enrolled him in school and his teacher called me in and said Joey doesn't partici-pate in class. He just sits there doing nothing, she said. I took him to Dr. Gibson to be sure he wasn't sick or something and that's how I ended up here."

"How well does Joey know you, Mr. Chandler?" Cedar asked.

"Call me Mark. My sister and I were close, talked on the phone at least once a week, but I couldn't get to New York much because of work. I visited for a couple of days last Christmas, but…Joey recognizes me when he sees me, but *know* me? I guess I'd have to say he doesn't really know me if that means feel-ing comfortable with me, or trusting me. I'm just Uncle Mark who showed up once in a while."

"Do *you* feel comfortable with him?"

Mark uncrossed his legs and shifted in his chair.

"Not…really," he said, a deep frown knitting his brow. "I don't have a clue what to say to him about his parents, or even about something as simple as how his day went. Dinner conversation is something like 'So, Joey, how'd school go today?' and he'll say ''kay' and that's it for the entire meal. Then he asks to be excused and spends the rest of the evening in his room until I tell him it's time for a bath and bed.''

"It sounds as though Joey has his emotions under lock and key," Cedar said.

"That's a good way to put it," Mark said, producing a small smile. "I'm doing a lousy job with him and I realize that. I need help here. It is November already and if Joey doesn't start doing some work at school, he's liable to flunk second grade. Plus there's so much tension in our house, you could cut it with a knife."

"All right," Cedar said. "I have the basic information I need to start working with Joey. I do need you to fill out this form for his file, though. I'd like to see him three times a week to start. Is he available after school?"

"Well, no, not exactly. A van takes him up from school to a day-care center, where I pick him up just before six when they close."

"That's a long day for a little boy," Cedar said.

"Yeah, well, I have a lot to do running Chandler Construction."

"We'll get into that later," Cedar said. "There will be times, Mr…Mark, when I'll want to see you alone, sessions when I want to see you and Joey together and, of course, sessions with Joey on his own. I also do things a bit differently than most child psychologists.

"I feel an office setting can be intimidating for my young clients, so I'll come to your home, or go on an outing with Joey, perhaps join you and Joey for dinner at a pizza parlor. We'll decide on those things further down the line."

"Whatever you say."

"Now about Joey's appointments. To have you bring him here after you pick him up at day care isn't workable. He'll be tired, hungry…no, I need you to get him here three times a week right after school."

"Man," Mark said, running one hand over the back of his neck. "Okay, yeah, I'll figure something out."

"Good." Cedar got to her feet holding the information form. "Let's go look at the appointment book and set up some of those sessions."

"There's one other thing I feel you should know," Mark said, rising.

"Yes?"

"Joey hasn't cried."

"What?"

"He hasn't cried through any of this."

"Are you certain of that?" Cedar said, joining him in front of her desk. "What about when he was at the neighbor's while you were tending to the estate?"

He shook his head. "Maggie, the neighbor, made a point of telling me that Joey didn't want to talk about his parents, nor did he cry if she or her kids brought up the subject. He didn't cry at the funeral, or when I brought him here or…no, Dr. Kennedy, Joey hasn't cried."

"Cedar is fine. I like to keep things casual, but goodness, Joey must address his pain, let his emotions out instead of bottling them up. For a seven year old to not have cried when his very world was destroyed is saying a great deal about his mental state."

"You sound…I don't know…like you really care about Joey and you haven't even met him yet."

"He's a child in crisis, Mark. Of course, I care."

"Do you have kids of your own?"

"No," Cedar said quietly. "I don't. My clients are my family. Oh, and my very spoiled cat Oreo."

"You don't have a husband or children, and you devote yourself to other people's kids who are messed up. That's admirable, but don't you get lonely at times?"

"Do you?" Cedar said, starting toward the office door.

"Ah-ha," Mark said, following her. "Now that was a slam-dunk shrinky-dink maneuver. You answered a question with a question."

"Of course," Cedar said, laughing. "We're taught that the very first week of classes in college."

"Whoa," Mark said, as they entered the reception area. "I thought your smile was something else, but your laughter is…is…okay, I'm going for corny here. Your laughter is like wind chimes. Nice, very nice."

"Thank you," Cedar mumbled, then glanced at her watch. "We'd better hurry. You fill out this form while I set up some appointments for Joey. You don't want to be late picking him up at the day-care center. Do you cook dinner for Joey?"

"Sort of. We eat a lot of scrambled eggs which is about it as far as my culinary skills go. We do the fast-food circuit and order in."

"Mmm," Cedar said, shaking her head. "We'll discuss that later, too."

Cedar scheduled appointments for Joey over the next two weeks while Mark filled out the form. She gave him a paper with the session dates and times, then offered him her hand.

"It was a pleasure to meet you," she said. "I'm looking forward to speaking with Joey."

Mark took her hand. "I appreciate your being willing to take him on."

Was that heat slithering up her arm and across her breasts? Cedar thought. Good heavens, it was.

Mark's hand was strong and callused, yet so gentle. His touch had caused a strange and disturbing feeling—

"May I have my hand back now?" she said.

"Oh. Sure," Mark said, releasing her hand very slowly. "Thanks again…Cedar."

"You're welcome…Mark."

When the door to the suite closed behind Mark Chandler, Cedar sank into Bethany's chair, propped her elbows on the desk and pressed her hands to her warm cheeks.

That man was dangerous. He radiated sensuality by merely entering a room with that loose-hipped walk of his. Add to that his height and build and chiseled features…gracious, he must have to beat off women with a stick.

Well, she was on guard now against the potent Mr. Chandler. He wouldn't fluster her again. She wouldn't allow that to happen. She'd just be more alert than she usually was against men.

The focus had to be Joey.

Poor, sad, devastated little Joey, who really, really needed to cry.

Chapter Two

As Cedar entered her house, she realized she had thought about Mark Chandler and Joey during the entire drive home. That was understandable, she decided, because Mark had been the last client she'd seen that day.

She'd read the form Mark had filled out and learned there were no other relatives on either side of Joey's family. It was just the two of them, uncle and nephew, and that combination was definitely not going well at the moment.

Cedar closed the door behind her and told herself

to leave her two new clients, Mark and Joey, on the porch that swept across the front of the house.

Over a year before she had purchased the old, two-story Victorian house. It had the charm and grace of a past era and she'd been captivated, imagining the marvelous stories the stately structure would tell if its walls could whisper.

In the year since signing the mortgage papers the charm of her home had greatly diminished. Although it had passed the initial inspection and was declared to be in excellent condition, she had spent the past fourteen months tending to one repair after another.

She was seriously considering selling the savings-draining house and buying something newer. However, since her reputation as a child psychologist was growing in Phoenix and more and more clients came under her care, there didn't seem to be a spare moment in her schedule to explore the market for something else.

Plus, the thought of packing and moving again was more than she could bear. For now she would stay put, but she had mental fingers crossed that the rash of repairs was at an end for a while.

"Oreo, I'm home. Come do your I'm-so-glad-to-see-you thing."

A large, black-and-white cat strolled into the room, then wove around her legs, meowing loudly.

Was this pathetic? Cedar thought. Was she becoming a classic spinster at thirty-two, coming home to a house that held nothing more than a fat cat to greet her?

Don't you get lonely at times?

The words Mark Chandler had spoken suddenly echoed in Cedar's mind and a shiver coursed through her. She reached down and picked up Oreo.

"Hello, pretty girl," Cedar said. "We're a good team, aren't we? We don't need anyone else living here with us and, no, we don't get lonely at times."

Oreo wiggled in Cedar's arms, then jumped to the floor and ran toward the kitchen.

"But the question remains," Cedar said, pointing a finger in the air, "as to whether you love me for me, Ms. Oreo, or because I'm the one who feeds you? Do I want to know the answer to that? No, I do not." She shook her head. "Isn't this super? Now I'm talking to myself, for Pete's sake."

Cedar went upstairs to change into soft, faded jeans and an equally worn Arizona State University sweatshirt. Returning to the main floor, she went into the kitchen, fed a complaining Oreo, then opened the refrigerator to see what might tempt her for dinner.

Mark could only make scrambled eggs, she thought. Why were men so quick to decide that their gender made it acceptable to be helpless in the kitchen? It was no longer politically correct to assume the attitude that cooking was woman's work. Mark should buy a cookbook and prepare nourishing, well-balanced meals for growing Joey. Cooking, in fact, was something the pair could tackle together, use as a bonding tool. She'd have to speak to Mark about that and—

"That's it, Mark Chandler," Cedar said aloud, as she took lettuce and a tomato from a shelf. "Go back to the front porch where I left you. Right now."

But Mark refused to budge.

He seemed to hover while Cedar prepared her meal of pasta with spicy sauce, a tossed salad and two slices of garlic bread.

He was at the table while Cedar consumed her dinner, then cleaned the kitchen. When she settled into her favorite easy chair that was big enough for two, he somehow managed to perch on the rounded arm of the chair.

Cedar snatched up the book on the table next to the chair, turned on the light and opened the book to where she'd left off the night before. After reading three paragraphs and realizing she hadn't understood one word, she snapped the book closed and frowned.

What on earth was going on here? she thought.

She'd had a date with a dentist a month ago and had forgotten he existed by the time he'd backed out of her driveway after bringing her home.

Why was Mark Chandler, who was a client and automatically not eligible for anything other than professional meetings, consuming her thoughts and managing to have such an intense affect on her? His presence was so palpable, she felt as though she could reach out and actually touch him right there in her living room.

Now there was an enticing image, Cedar mused. Touching Mark Chandler. She had a feeling the chest beneath that faded shirt was rock-solid, as were his arms and those long, long legs. His thick hair just called to feminine fingers to sift through it, then watch it glide back into place. His lips—

"Aakk," Cedar yelled, as Oreo jumped into the chair and startled her back to reality. "Oh, good grief, Oreo, you scared the bejeebers out of me. But I deserve it because I had no business thinking what I was and…Oreo, give it to me straight. Am I losing it?

"Nothing like this has ever happened to me before and it's disconcerting to say the least. I mean, really, Mark Chandler isn't even my type, you know what I mean? I go for the suit-and-tie guys, not dust-covered construction…dudes. So why is Mark capable of consuming my brain and…"

Oreo leaped over the arm of the chair and left the room.

Cedar sighed. "That went well. This whole situation is so ridiculous, my own cat decided it wasn't worth listening to.

"Okay, I'm on my own. This is Thursday. I see Mark again on Monday when he brings Joey for his appointment. Between now and then I'll get it together and knock off this nonsense. Yes, I will, because I am woman...in charge, in control."

Cedar opened the book to the proper page and began to read, extremely glad there wouldn't be a test later on what she was supposedly comprehending.

Mark straightened the blanket over a sleeping Joey, then left the toy-strewn bedroom. He wandered down the hall to the large living room and slouched into a well-worn chair he refused to have reupholstered. Picking up the remote from the end table, he clicked on the television, only to be greeted by canned laughter. He shut it off again.

It had been another silent evening in the Chandler household, he thought dismally. No matter how hard he'd tried, he couldn't get Joey to respond to his chatty questions with more than one-word answers. Joey had just stared at him with those big, dark and so damn sad eyes of his and Mark had finally given up and allowed the kid to finish his scrambled eggs in a silence that seemed to weigh a ton.

"Ah, hell." Mark dragged his hands down his face, then laced them on his chest.

Mary had trusted him with her son, Mark thought dismally. He and Mary had been so close, and he missed her. At times he caught himself reaching for the phone to call her and hear her cheerful voice. She'd be devastated if she knew how unhappy Joey was in his new home with his Uncle Mark, and disappointed in her brother for being such a lousy father.

"Ah, hell," he said again.

He'd spent more than one evening sitting here mentally beating himself up because he couldn't break through the walls that sad little boy had built around himself. Well, now things were different. He'd taken a positive step toward getting help for Joey by seeing Cedar Kennedy.

Cedar.

He liked her name. It was unique and had a nice ring to it. And he liked her smile and her dynamite wind-chime laughter. Her hair was pretty, framing her delicate features with soft blond waves and… Why wasn't a woman like that married? How stupid and blind were the men in Phoenix, for crying out loud?

Maybe she hated men. Why would she hate men? Had she been badly hurt in the past by some jerk? That was a disturbing thought. He'd like to pop that guy right in the chops for…no, he was getting carried away here. He didn't have a clue why Cedar Kennedy wasn't married.

Maybe she'd been too busy establishing her career, just as he had been, to become involved in a serious relationship. That made sense. He'd come right out and asked her if she ever got lonely and she'd thrown that question right back in his lap.

Did he get lonely?

What difference did that make anyway? He didn't have enough hours in the day to do all that needed tending at Chandler Construction and now he had become an instant father of a little boy who was so miserable, it was enough to break a person's heart.

Well, come Monday, things were going to be different once he placed Joey in Cedar's care. He'd do whatever Cedar recommended.

Except what had she meant by saying they'd talk later about his lack of cooking skills? Hey, eggs were good for a kid and there was nothing wrong with hamburgers and pizza.

Cedar. He was definitely looking forward to seeing her again on Monday. She was, he hoped, the solution to Joey's unhappiness, and he was eager to get this show on the road. His anticipation didn't really have anything to do with Cedar the woman, no matter how attractive she was. Or how her smile lit up her face, or her laughter.

"Enough," Mark said, pressing the remote to bring the television to life. "Watch the news, Chandler, and quit thinking."

"I suppose you want me to give up my baby for adoption just like everyone else. Well, I won't. I don't care what you say, I won't."

Cedar looked at the sullen fifteen year old who sat opposite her desk. "I didn't suggest that at all," she said gently. "I simply asked how you planned to provide for your child, Cindy."

"I'll manage," Cindy said, then began to nibble on one of her fingernails.

"How do you feel about the baby's father leaving town when you told him you were pregnant?"

"I don't need him," Cindy said, dropping her hand to her rounded stomach. "I made a mistake by thinking he loved me, but it's no big deal. He'd be a crummy father anyway."

"But you're not making a mistake by insisting that you can manage to raise a child on your own, without a high-school education?" Cedar said.

"No. I'll get a job. I can wait tables, or whatever.

Waitresses make good tips if they're nice to the customers. And I'll get a cute little apartment and fix it up really nice. I've done a lot of babysitting, you know, so I can take care of my baby just fine. It's not as though I haven't thought this through. I know what I'm doing."

Cedar nodded. "Okay. I'm going to give you an assignment I'd like you to complete before we meet again next Monday."

"Oh, bogus," Cindy said, rolling her eyes heavenward. "What is it?"

"I want you to look in the newspaper for apartments, then enquire about how much money you'll need to move into a place of your own…such as first and last month's rent, security deposit, the whole nine yards. Then I want you to find out what waitress jobs are paying these days. Also, call several day-care centers and ask about their rates.

"You do that much, then we'll work together to figure out the additional cost of diapers, formula, utilities, transportation and on the list goes. Now, before you start to argue with me about this, remember you signed a contract stating that you would cooperate with me one hundred percent."

"Yeah, right, okay," Cindy mumbled.

"Good. I'm sure your foster mother is in the waiting room because our time is up," Cedar said, getting to her feet. "I'll see you in a week. We'll meet here again, then in the future let's consider getting together in a park or a cozy café."

"Whatever," Cindy said, then rose and stomped across the office, closing the door behind her with a resounding thud.

"Oh, Cindy," Cedar said, sinking back into her chair. "I'm sorry, sweetie, but I'm going to burst your bubble."

Cedar opened Cindy Swanson's file and wrote notes from the session with the pregnant teenager.

Cindy's divorced mother had four younger children at home. When Cindy had announced that she was pregnant, the mother couldn't deal with it. She'd called Child Protective Services and had Cindy placed in foster care. CPS had then made arrangements for Cindy to become one of Cedar's clients. Beyond the many cases the social service organization had directed to her, she also got referrals from schools and private physicians…like the one who had recommended her to Mark Chandler.

Mark Chandler, who was no doubt sitting in the waiting room right now with Joey.

Mark Chandler, who hadn't strayed far from her thoughts the entire weekend, the rotten bum.

Cedar placed Cindy's file in the out basket for Bethany to file, then reached in another basket for

Joey's file and placed it on her desk. She stood, tugged on the hem of the navy blazer she wore with a red blouse over winter-white slacks, then walked slowly across the room. She drew a steadying breath before opening the door.

Cedar felt, and tried to ignore the immediate increased tempo of her heart as she looked at Mark sitting on a sofa against the far wall. When she shifted her gaze to the small boy next to him, her heart did a funny little two-step.

Joey. He looked enough like Mark to be his son, with his tousled black hair and big, dark eyes. He appeared small for his age, his feet not reaching the floor.

Even with the distance between them she could sense Joey's vulnerability and wanted to scoop him up, hug him and tell him everything was going to be just fine.

Objectivity, Dr. Kennedy, Cedar told herself, then crossed the room to stand in front of the pair.

"Hello, Mark," she said, smiling. "And you must be Joey. I've been eager to meet you."

Joey glanced up at her, then quickly directed his attention to his hands that were clutched tightly in his lap.

"Say hello, Joey," Mark said.

"'Lo," Joey mumbled.

"I'd like to chat with you a bit, Joey," Cedar said,

extending one hand toward the little boy. "Shall we go into my office? We'll let your Uncle Mark stay out here and finish reading his magazine."

"No," Joey said.

"Hey, buddy, we talked about this," Mark said. "I'll be right here waiting for you, I promise. You go with Dr. Kennedy."

"Call me Cedar, Joey," she said.

Joey frowned and looked up at her. "That's a weird name."

"Oh, cripe," Mark said, shaking his head. "Joey, you don't tell someone that their name is weird."

"Well, it is," Joey said.

Cedar laughed. "It's different, that's for sure. It was my mother's last name before she got married. She thought by sharing it with me, it would connect us in a special way."

"Is your mom dead?" Joey asked.

"No, she isn't," Cedar said. "She and my father live in Florida now. I miss them very much."

Joey folded his thin little arms over his chest. "You'd miss them more if they were dead people 'cause you couldn't talk to them on the phone or nothing. Nothing."

"I never thought of that," Cedar said. "Let's go into my office and you can explain it to me further."

Joey slid off the sofa, but ignored Cedar's outstretched hand. Cedar smiled at Mark, but he just shook his head again, a frown on his face.

"Did Joey get a snack, Bethany?" Cedar said. "Busy boys are hungry after school."

"He certainly did," Bethany said. "He had a juice box and a granola bar." Her secretary was a plump woman in her early fifties, who was in the process of consuming her own box of juice and a granola bar.

"Good," Cedar said, then placed her hand lightly on Joey's back and guided him into her office, shutting the door behind them.

In the office Cedar patted the seat of one of the chairs fronting her desk, then sat down in the other one once Joey was settled.

"How come you're not sitting behind your desk like the principal or something?" Joey said.

"I like to sit here when I'm getting to know a new friend." Cedar paused. "Joey, would you like to talk some more about how you can't speak with your parents on the telephone?"

"No," he said, drumming his fingers on his thighs and watching the repeated motion.

"Okay. So, tell me, do you like your teacher at school?"

Joey shrugged.

"Have you made some new friends?"

Joey shrugged.

"Are you getting along all right with your Uncle Mark?"

Joey shrugged.

"Are you tired of eating scrambled eggs?"

Joey's head snapped up. "Those eggs are so gross. They're never good. Sometimes they run all over my plate and sometimes they're hard as a rock and...I hate scrambled eggs the way Uncle Mark cooks them. Totally, totally gross."

Cedar nodded. "They do sound gross. Have you told Uncle Mark you'd rather not have scrambled eggs anymore?"

"No. No, 'cause he...he might get mad at me or something and tell me I can't live with him, and I don't have anywhere else to live because...because I don't."

"Because your parents were killed in the accident?" Cedar said gently.

"That's none of your business," Joey yelled.

"Okay. Let's go back to discussing those gross scrambled eggs. I'll make a deal with you."

Joey narrowed his eyes. "Like what?"

"I'll be the one to tell your Uncle Mark you'd rather not have scrambled eggs again. I guarantee that he won't get angry about it."

"Bet he will. He's grumpy."

"We'll see," Cedar said. "I'll do that for you, but

you have to do something for me. That's how this deal works."

"What do I have to do?"

"Well, if you don't want gross eggs, we have to decide what you *do* want, then teach Uncle Mark how to make it. You invite me to your house and we'll give him a cooking lesson. That's your part of the deal. You invite me over and we, together, show Uncle Mark how to make your choice and tell him it can't be gross when he does it. How's that? What would you like to eat instead of scrambled eggs?"

Joey shrugged.

"Well, I guess you're stuck with gross eggs then."

"No, wait," Joey said. "I'd rather have chicken with barbecue sauce. I really like that. But Uncle Mark can't ever learn how to make it. No way. He got a big fat chicken one time and stuck it in a pan without barbecue sauce on it or nothing, just a fat naked chicken and we waited for it to cook and stuff, you know? I was really hungry and hours went by and then Uncle Mark figured out he didn't turn on the stove right and the stupid chicken was just sitting there. Cold. I mean, that is so dumb."

Cedar laughed. "So what did you have for dinner? No, let me guess. Gross scrambled eggs."

A hint of a smile appeared on Joey's face, then disappeared in the next instant.

"Yeah," he said. "Eggs again."

"Okay, my new friend. We're in business. I'll buy what we need to make barbecue chicken, bring it to your house, and you and I will show Uncle Mark how to fix it."

"He'll never go for this," Joey said, rolling his eyes.

"Let's find out," Cedar said, getting to her feet. "I'll go get him."

"He's going to be really, really grumpy," Joey said, then sighed.

Cedar opened the office door. "Mark? Would you come in please?"

"Yeah. Sure," he said, getting to his feet and hurrying across the room. "How's it going?"

"Joey and I have something of great importance to discuss with you."

"Already?" Mark said, raising his eyebrows. "Hey, that's terrific."

"Mark, you take the chair opposite Joey and I'll sit behind my desk now," Cedar said.

Mark settled onto the chair and looked at Cedar, an expression of anticipation on his face.

"Joey and I have talked at length," she said, "and I have agreed to be the spokesperson here."

"I'm listening, believe me," Mark said, leaning forward.

"Mark," Cedar said seriously, "you make extremely gross scrambled eggs."

"I...what?"

"Yes. Totally gross," Cedar said. "Joey would prefer not to eat the scrambled eggs you prepare. Ever again."

"What?" Mark repeated.

"So, Joey and I are going to teach you how to make what he would *like* to eat. Barbecue chicken."

"*This* is the matter of great importance that you wanted to discuss with me?" Mark said, none too quietly.

"I told you, I told you," Joey said, stiffening in his chair. "He's getting grumpy right now. See? He is."

"I am not grumpy," Mark said, then cleared his throat. "I'm...I'm just a bit surprised about the subject, that's all. My eggs are gross, Joey?"

"The worst," Joey said. "Totally."

"I didn't think they were that bad," Mark said, frowning. "They wouldn't win first place in an egg-cooking contest, but...you want barbecue chicken? I didn't have much luck with that other chicken, remember?"

"Yeah, well, this time Cedar and me are going to show you how to do barbecue chicken right," Joey said. "Then you'll know how to do barbecue chicken and gross eggs will be history."

"Got it," Mark said, a bemused expression on his face.

"What evening this week would be good for you?" Cedar asked. She flipped through her engagement calendar. "We'll cancel our Wednesday afternoon appointment. I'm free Thursday or Friday."

"Pick one," Mark said, throwing up his hands.

"Friday night?" Cedar said, then recorded it. "I'll be at your house by five-thirty."

"But I work until…" Mark hesitated. "Five-thirty, it is."

"Good," she said. "Joey, it was wonderful to meet you and I am really looking forward to cooking with you and enjoying that chicken. I'll see you Friday night. Why don't you go see Bethany now and tell her I said you could pick a piece of candy from the jar. I want to speak to your Uncle Mark for a second."

"'Kay," Joey said, then slid off the chair and ran out of the office.

Cedar leaned forward and folded her hands on her desk. "Mark, I am so pleased with the progress made today with Joey," she said, smiling.

"You are?" he said. "Pardon my confusion, but I thought you two were coming in here to discuss Joey's parents. But the topic was my crummy eggs? Why are we thrilled?"

"Because Joey and I are establishing a rapport. He was comfortable enough with me to tell me that he wished he didn't have to eat those scrambled eggs."

Mark got to his feet. "Why didn't he just tell *me?*"

"Mark, you have to understand where Joey is coming from. He is a bright little boy who realizes that you are the only person available to provide a home for him. He's lost his parents. He's now terrified that if he upsets you, you won't want him to live with you."

"That's nuts," Mark said, nearly shouting.

"Shh," Cedar said, rising to round the desk. "I don't want Joey to hear any of this. He used me as a buffer to deliver the message about the eggs and to inform you what he does like to eat. It's a marvelous start. Our Friday session will also give me a chance to see his bedroom, the possessions that are important to him, and to watch the interaction between you and Joey.

"Joey's problems are not going to be solved overnight. It will be a slow process. He did not want to discuss his parents with me, and I didn't push him on the subject. I have to establish a level of trust with Joey first. And…well, I need you to trust me, too."

Mark looked at Cedar for a long moment.

"Doesn't that work both ways?" he said finally. "Don't *you* need to trust *me?*"

"I don't understand what you mean."

"You're going to be coming to my home, plus you said we'd be going on outings together with Joey at times. We'll also have private meetings such as this one right now to discuss progress. I'm referring to you trusting me as a man, not just as Joey's guardian. Do you trust me as a man?"

"I…" Cedar stopped speaking.

Why was Mark doing this? she thought frantically. She didn't intend to view him as a *man*. No, he was Joey's guardian, his uncle, the person who was now that little boy's father. Their relationship had nothing to do with Cedar, the woman, trusting Mark, the man.

Mark Chandler unsettled her, made her acutely aware of her own femininity and his incredible masculinity. She had no idea if she trusted him. She was having enough trouble trusting *herself* not to overreact to his blatant sensuality whenever she was near him, for heaven's sake.

"Your question is immaterial, Mark," she said, tearing her gaze from his.

"I don't believe it is," he said. "How is Joey going to relax around me if he senses tension between you and me? How will he come to trust me if he feels that you don't? Think about it."

"I…"

"You have my address on that form I filled out.

Joey and I will be waiting for your arrival Friday night. We'll all cook dinner together, just like a family. Right? Right." Mark nodded. "See ya."

Mark strode from the room. Cedar sank into one of the chairs in front of her desk when she realized her trembling legs were not going to support her for one second longer.

This was *not* going well, she thought, pressing her hands to her flushed cheeks. Mark had made a legitimate point. Joey *would* be aware of any tension between her and Mark and might very well hold back because of it.

She had to somehow gain control of her raging emotions before Friday night. She was a professional. She'd taken part in in-home therapy a multitude of times and found it to be very effective and informative. She would concentrate on Joey and the chicken, and view Mark as the client that he was. *Not a man...a client.*

She could do that.

Couldn't she?

Chapter Three

On Friday evening before Cedar arrived, Mark stood in the middle of his living room and nodded in approval. He had made a fire in the hearth that was now crackling with leaping flames. The cleaning lady, who came three times a week, had done her usual expert job.

Mark had built the large house in Fountain Valley, an affluent area at the north edge of Phoenix. The split floor plan featured a master bedroom on one side of the house and three more bedrooms on the opposite side. There were also a sunken living room with a flagstone fireplace, a formal dining room, a big kitchen with an eating area, and a library with built-in shelves.

The backyard boasted a swimming pool, plus a separate Jacuzzi beyond a good-size covered patio.

Mark had hired a decorator who had chosen large, comfortable furniture in tones of gray and light-to-dark burgundy. The overall effect was one of simple elegance.

He had known when he designed and built the house that it was much too big for a single man, but he'd had hopes of having a wife and children someday and wanted to be prepared. He'd also intended to establish a sizable investment portfolio that would provide not only for his retirement, but for college educations for his children. He wanted available funds for any emergencies that might arise.

One had.

Until Joey's arrival, the three spare bedrooms had been empty. Together, they had shopped for Joey's furniture, which had proven to be a study in frustration, as Joey offered no opinions and answered most questions with his ever-familiar shrug.

Wanting Joey to have his own possessions with him, Mark had his nephew's clothes, toys, and books shipped from New York. He had even purchased a Game Boy as a gift for Joey, but had yet to see the little boy play with it.

Cedar would see that Joey had a nice home.

Joey's new bedroom was large and had its own bathroom. It contained a double bed, dresser, desk, and bookshelves to hold his belongings. Everything that a little boy could possibly want was available under this roof.

Yeah, right, Mark thought, shaking his head. It all sounded great except for the fact that Joey was a very unhappy kid. The easy way out would be to blame Joey's emotional state entirely on the loss of his parents. That might very well be true, but Cedar would need to make that determination.

"No, part of it is me," Mark said, frowning.

He was doing a lousy job of being a father, no doubt about it. He should be able to get Joey to smile, for Pete's sake, to talk to him, to spend just one evening with his Uncle Mark.

Hell, what did *he* know about being a dad? Not a damn thing. He sure hadn't had any kind of role model. Not even close. Should he tell Cedar that? Explain his own childhood to her so she could understand why he was doing such a crummy job of—no. He wasn't about to pour out his heart and soul to a woman he hardly knew. No way.

The doorbell rang, jerking Mark from his rambling thoughts. As he started across the room, Joey came running down the hall and entered the living room.

"Cedar's here," Joey said, zooming to the door. He flung it open just as Mark reached him.

"Hi, Cedar," Joey said. "Did you bring the chicken and stuff?"

"I certainly did," Cedar said, smiling. "Are you ready to be a chef?"

"Yeah," Joey said. "Cool."

"Joey," Mark said, "why don't you invite Cedar in?"

"Huh?" Joey said. "Oh. You wanna come in now?"

Cedar laughed. "Yes, thank you." She stepped into the living room and swept her gaze over the large expanse. "What a lovely home," she said. "Oh, and a fire in the hearth. Perfect." She looked at Joey again. "Would you take one of these grocery sacks, please?"

"Sure," Joey said, slamming the door closed, then accepting one of the bags.

Cedar hadn't acknowledged his presence or even glanced in his direction, Mark thought. So, okay, she was here in her role as Joey's psychologist, but still—

Man, listen to him. He was reacting like a bratty little kid who was jealous because the new baby was getting all the attention. But, cripe, the woman could at least say hello.

"Hello, Cedar," he said.

Cedar slowly, very slowly, shifted her gaze to meet Mark's.

"Hello, Mark," she said.

"Let me take that other sack," he said, reaching toward it.

"Oh, it's fine," Cedar said.

"I insist," he said, then grasped the bag, the back of his right hand brushing her breast lightly. "Oh, excuse me. I didn't mean to…sorry."

"Apology accepted," Cedar said. "On to the kitchen, gentlemen."

Providing that her legs would carry her that far, she thought frantically, which was doubtful because her bones were dissolving from the incredible heat that was consuming her. That one-second flicker of Mark's hand on her breast was wreaking total havoc on her body.

There was a flush on her cheeks, too, she just knew there was, darn it. This evening was *not* starting out well at all.

"Are you coming?" Joey said from across the room.

"What?" Cedar said. "Oh, yes, of course. Lead the way, sir."

In the kitchen, Cedar offered the appropriate compliments on the state-of-the-art appliances and the generous size of the room, finally deciding that she was babbling like an idiot.

"Okay," she said, then drew a steadying breath. "First thing we do is wash our hands."

As they all turned toward the double sink, Cedar was acutely aware that Mark was behind her...very, very close behind her.

"I'll go first and get out of the way," she said quickly.

Oh, Cedar, she admonished herself, as she dried her hands on a towel. Would you please get it together before you make a complete fool of yourself?

She reached into one of the sacks now sitting on the counter and removed a bright blue square of material.

"This is your chef's apron, Joey," she said. "All famous chefs wear aprons, you know." She shook it out to reveal the bright orange Garfield the Cat on the front. "How's this?"

"Cool," Joey said.

Cedar slipped the apron over Joey's head and tied it in the back.

"I don't want to get stuff on it," Joey said.

"That's what aprons are for, sweetie," Cedar said. "It doesn't matter if it gets messy."

"Yes, it does," he said, nearly shouting. "'Cause then it will be yucky, and you might tell me to throw it away or something, and I won't have it anymore, and it will be gone forever."

"Hey, buddy," Mark said, "calm down. You can keep the apron even if it gets stained."

"Promise?" Joey said.

"Promise," Mark said.

"Well…okay then," Joey said.

He's so fragile, Cedar thought, her heart seeming to melt as she looked at Joey, who was smoothing the front of the apron. *It will be gone forever.* He'd lost his parents and couldn't bear the idea of losing anything else, not even a gaudy little apron. Oh, Joey.

Cedar looked at Mark over the top of Joey's head and their gazes met, his expression telling her that he'd understood the meaning of Joey's outburst.

"There's a lot of work to be done here," Cedar said, still looking directly at Mark.

"No joke," Mark said, frowning.

"Yeah, we gotta cook a big ol' dinner," Joey said. "Are you gonna write stuff down, Uncle Mark?"

"What?" Mark said. "Oh, sure, you bet."

The project began.

With Joey kneeling on a chair next to Cedar, the chicken was rinsed, placed on a baking sheet, then coated with barbecue sauce that Joey spread with a butter knife with exacting care.

Potatoes were scrubbed, punctured with a fork, then wrapped in foil and placed on the second shelf of the oven below the tray of chicken.

As delicious aromas began to waft through the air, a tossed salad was prepared and sprinkled with Italian dressing.

Mark made a big production of writing down the directions for all that was being done as Cedar chatted with Joey. She learned the name of his teacher, that he liked science but hated math, that lunch in the cafeteria was sorta gross but not too bad some days, and that girls were weird but there was a boy named Benny who might be his friend but maybe not.

"Benny has a mom, but not a dad," Joey said, as he folded paper napkins, "'cause last year his dad said he liked a different lady better than Benny's mom and they live far away now and stuff. He sent Benny a card with five dollars in it once."

"Is Benny sad because his dad isn't with him anymore?" Cedar said, as she carried silverware to the table.

Joey shrugged. "Sometimes, I guess. But I told him that having his dad far away was better than having his dad be dead forever."

Oh, man, listen to him, Mark thought, as he placed glasses on the table. A seven year old shouldn't be thinking about things like that, but at least he was talking. Joey had said more to Cedar during the preparation of this meal than he had during all the weeks he'd lived here. Cedar Kennedy was obviously very good at what she did.

She was also very good at pushing his sexual buttons by doing nothing more than being in the same room with him. She looked sensational in her snug jeans and bright red sweater. And when she smiled, or laughed, he could feel the heat coil low in his body, driving him right up the wall. She wasn't trying to get a reaction from him, he knew that. It was just happening because…well, because she was Cedar.

"I think you're being a very good friend to Benny," Cedar said.

"He *might* be my friend," Joey said. "Friends should be friends forever, you know? I don't want to ask Benny to promise that 'cause…I just don't."

"Why don't you just be friends one day at a time?" Cedar said. "Don't worry about forever, just have fun with Benny each day as it comes for now."

"Maybe."

"Let's check the chicken, sir chef," Cedar said, ruffling Joey's hair.

Dinner was delicious and praise was directed to the little chef who beamed.

"Do you have a kid?" Joey asked Cedar as they ate.

"Hey, buddy," Mark said, "that's kind of a personal question to ask someone."

"It's fine, Mark," she said, then took a bite of fluffy potato. "No, Joey. I don't have a child. I was married once, but I'm not married now."

"How come?" Joey said.

Mark realized he was waiting for Cedar's answer as intently as Joey was.

"Because sometimes, even though we want things to be forever, it just doesn't work out that way," she said quietly. "It makes us very sad when that happens, but we have to learn to smile again and look forward to all the adventures yet to come. Understand?"

Joey shrugged.

"I really cried a lot when I knew I wasn't going to be married forever," Cedar continued. "It may sound strange, Joey, but crying when you're sad can actually make you feel better."

Joey shrugged.

"Do you have room in your tummy for another piece of chicken, Joey?" Cedar said. "Yes? No? Maybe you'll want to leave room for the chocolate chip ice cream I brought."

"Do you like being in your house all by yourself?" Joey said.

"Oh, I'm not alone," Cedar said, smiling. "I have

a cat named Oreo. I named her that because she's black and white."

"Cats are cool," Joey said, nodding in approval.

"I sure like being in this house better since you came to live with me, Joey," Mark said. "Having you here beats being all by myself."

"Really?" Joey said, his eyes widening.

"Yep," Mark said. "I wish you'd talk to me more, though."

"Well, I might be able to do that," Joey said. "Maybe."

"I'd appreciate it," Mark said.

"Cedar could live here with us and bring her cat Oreo," Joey said, "in case I don't want to talk to you too much, Uncle Mark."

Interesting thought, Mark mused, stifling a chuckle. How was Cedar going to respond to *that* one?

"Do you have room for that ice cream, Joey?" Cedar said.

Mark laughed. "There's more than one kind of chicken at this table, Dr. Kennedy."

"Huh?" Joey said.

Cedar glared at Mark.

After they'd consumed ice cream and cleaned the kitchen, Cedar asked Joey if he'd like to show her his room.

"It's just a room, with a bed and stuff," Joey said. "There's nothing much to see or anything."

"But you have—" Mark started.

"Well, maybe another time," Cedar interrupted.

"Yeah…maybe," Joey said. "I need to take my chef's apron off now. I hardly got anything messy on it."

Cedar helped him to remove the apron.

"Yep, you kept it pretty clean, Joey," she said, holding it up for view, "but I think it still needs to be washed."

"No," he said, snatching the apron out of Cedar's hands.

"Hey, that was rude," Mark said. "You shouldn't grab things from people, Joey."

Joey hugged the apron tightly. "But I don't want it washed. I'm going to go put it in a special place in my room and nobody can touch it but me. It's mine. Mine."

"That's fine," Cedar said. "Off you go to select that special place. I'm headed for the living room to enjoy that lovely fire."

Joey ran from the kitchen and Cedar walked slowly to the living room, Mark following behind her. She sank onto a love seat facing the fireplace while Mark put another log on the glowing embers. He straightened, rested one arm on the mantel and looked at her.

"I don't have a clue whether this evening is going well or not," he said, frowning. "Joey said more to you than he's ever said to me, but…are we thrilled or discouraged?"

Cedar smiled up at him. "Neither, really. I'm just gathering information."

"You approached some heavy topics, then backed off right away."

"It's like planting seeds, Mark. Now we wait to see if Joey thinks about any of those topics we touched on. He did to a point, when he broached the subject of my being alone. You did very well with that, by the way, by telling him you liked having him here." Cedar sighed. "Joey is a very frightened boy. He's even afraid to be friends with Benny because, to him, friendship is supposed to be forever, and Joey has no trust in forever anymore. We've got a long way to go with that little sweetheart."

"What about you, Cedar?" Mark said. "You didn't get happily ever after in your marriage. Have *you* learned to trust forever again?"

"I'm focused on my career now," she said, shifting her gaze to the flames in the hearth. "I really don't have time for a relationship. You should be able to relate to that. You obviously put in very long hours at your construction company."

"True, but someday, when I've reached my goals,

I want to have a wife and family. That won't be for quite a while yet, though." The wife part, at least. "I have a son, family, even if Joey isn't exactly thrilled about it."

"Well, I hope those goals are clearly defined in your mind," Cedar said, looking at Mark again, "so you know when you're there. Me? I'm centered totally on my career so I don't have to worry about when to shift gears."

"In other words, you don't trust in forever anymore," Mark said.

"I didn't say that," she said, lifting her chin. "I've chosen what I want to do with my life and I'm very content with my decision."

"Mmm," Mark said, then looked toward a hallway. "I don't think Joey is going to come back out of his room. I'm going to go get him. It's one thing to ignore me every evening, but you're company, and he's not being polite."

Cedar got to her feet. "No, let him do what feels right. I'll go say goodbye to him, but I won't attempt to enter his room because he doesn't want to share his private space yet."

"You're leaving?" Mark said, pushing away from the mantel. "There's no reason for you to go so soon. I mean, hey, shouldn't you be here in case Joey decides to be sociable? Anyway, just because Joey's had enough of our company for tonight doesn't mean *we* can't enjoy ourselves. I have a lot of DVDs if you'd like to watch a movie. I've even got some girl flicks that belonged to my sister. You know, like *Sleepless in Seattle* and *While You Were Sleeping* and *Casablanca.*"

"Girl flicks?" Cedar said, with a burst of laughter. "Oh, that is such a politically incorrect term, Mr. Chandler. Shame on you."

Mark grinned. "Well, what would you call those movies? I can't picture myself rushing out and buying any of them." He placed one hand over his heart. "However, nice guy that I am, I'll watch one with you."

"Thank you, but no," Cedar said, still smiling. "It's been a long day. I'd probably doze off halfway through a movie."

"No problem," Mark said, matching her smile. "That would mean you'd still be here in the morning and you could sample some of my world-famous scrambled eggs."

"Oh, I'm definitely going home now," Cedar said, laughing again.

The smile on Mark's face vanished.

"I told you how much I like hearing your laughter," he said, "but it bears repeating. Wind chimes." He stopped speaking, stared down at the floor for a long moment, then looked directly into Cedar's eyes. "You know, I realize you're here tonight for Joey, but I want to tell you that I enjoyed your company very much."

"Thank you, Mark," Cedar said. "I…I had a nice time, too, even though I was working, per se. But… well, I'm going to say good night to Joey and be on my way. I want to get home and make some notes on what took place with Joey while everything is fresh in my mind and add them to his file on Monday. My professional duties aren't over yet for today."

"You put in longer hours than I do, and I've been called a workaholic."

"I love what I do."

"But is it enough to fulfill the woman as well as the psychologist?" Mark said, raising his eyebrows.

"We've been over this ground, Mark," Cedar said. "I'm centered on my career. Now if you'll excuse me, I'll go see Joey."

Cedar hurried across the room and went down the hall, stopping at a closed door with a sliver of light visible at the bottom. She knocked. A moment later, Joey opened the door.

"I just wanted to say good night, Joey," Cedar said, smiling. "Thank you for a lovely evening and for cooking such a delicious dinner. I enjoyed being with you very much."

"'Kay," Joey said. "Did you like being with Uncle Mark, too?"

"Sure. He's a nice man. You might consider spending more time with him, instead of being alone in your room. Think about that. Okay?"

"'Kay. Bye. Thank you for my chef's apron, Cedar. I'm going to keep it…keep it…forever."

"I'm glad you like it. I'll see you at my office on Monday."

Joey nodded, then stepped back and closed the door.

Cedar stood in the hallway for a long moment, sending mental messages to Joey just to let go and cry, to bury his sad little face in his pillow and weep until he had no more tears to shed.

She sighed, then walked slowly to the living room to retrieve her purse from the chair where she'd placed it. She'd been so deeply in thought, she hadn't been aware that Mark had moved to stand close beside her.

"Mark," she said, "I'd like to ask you a personal question which you don't have to answer if you prefer not to."

"That sounds ominous, but ask away."

"When your sister and brother-in-law died in that accident, did *you* cry?"

Mark frowned. "Why would you want to know that?"

"Because if you did, and if the opportunity presented itself, you could tell Joey that there's nothing wrong with men crying when they're sad and that you're not ashamed about your tears. Maybe Joey's father preached the old philosophy 'real men don't cry' and that is playing a major role in Joey's refusal to shed those very important tears."

"Oh." Mark shoved his hands in the pockets of his jeans, yanked them out again, then stared at the ceiling, his shoes, anywhere but at Cedar. "Well, I…well, yeah… I cried because I was really busted up about what had happened, but…I don't think my telling Joey that would be helpful at all."

Cedar placed one hand on Mark's upper arm. "Oh, but it would be helpful," she said. "And it would mean far more than me, a woman, telling him that crying when you're sad is perfectly fine."

"No, Cedar, you don't get it. It was *not* easy to let go like that. I guess I made up my mind when I was a kid that tears sure as hell weren't going to change the crummy stuff that I was dealing with, so what was the point?"

"Crummy stuff?"

Mark waved one hand in the air in a dismissive gesture, causing Cedar to drop her hand back to her side.

"That's not important now," Mark said. "It's old

news best forgotten. We're talking about Joey's baggage, not mine. What I'm trying to say is that the only way I could cry for Mary and John was to…was to get drunk as a skunk. I really don't think you want me to give Joey a shot of whiskey and tell him to wail his little heart out."

"You had to get drunk before you could…" Cedar shook her head. "The fact that it's perfectly acceptable for men to show their emotions is being realized in our society much, much too late. Better late than never, I guess. Still… I'm sorry that you had what was apparently a less than wonderful childhood. I'm sorry that you have to get drunk to cry."

"Don't go there, Cedar," Mark said, shaking his head. "I don't intend to talk about it…ever." He paused. "So…you believe that a man should show his feelings."

"Yes. Yes, I do."

"That's good," he said. "That's very, very good, because I have this heavy-duty *feeling* that I need to kiss you." He framed her face with his hands, then lowered his head to claim her lips.

No, no, no, Cedar thought. This wasn't what she'd meant when she said…when she'd talked about—what had she been talking about? Oh, forget it. She really didn't care, because this kiss… mercy, this kiss…

Cedar's purse dropped unnoticed to the floor as she encircled Mark's shoulders with her arms. She returned his kiss in total abandon, savoring his taste, his aroma of soap and wood smoke, his strength tempered with infinite gentleness.

Oh, Mark, yes.

Oh, Cedar, no, said a niggling little voice in her brain. What on earth are you doing? This is wrong. Wrong, wrong, wrong.

She pushed on the hard wall of Mark's chest with enough force that he broke the kiss. He looked at her questioningly as he dropped his hands from her face.

"Wrong," she said, then took a much-needed breath. "That should not have happened."

"Why not?" he said, his voice slightly gritty. "You enjoyed that kiss as much as I did, and you know it. It was sensational, and you know it. There's no reason to say it was wrong, and you know it. So why are you saying it?"

"Because I don't go around kissing my clients, that's why," Cedar said, leaning down to snatch her purse from the floor.

"Well," Mark said, dragging a hand through his hair, "didn't that sound snooty as hell? Did you make that up, or is it in chapter whatever in one of your textbooks?"

"There's no call to be rude," Cedar said, with an indignant little sniff.

"Then don't go into shrinky-dink mode," Mark said, his volume rising. "That kiss was between a man and a woman, and you gave as good as you got. It had nothing to do with us being doctor and client. It was just you and me, Cedar, and it was dynamite."

"Yes, well, that's beside the point," she said, fiddling with the clasp on her purse. "I just want you to understand that it must not, will not, happen again."

"We'll see," Mark said, smiling.

"Good night, Mark," Cedar said, glaring at him.

"Good night, Cedar," he said, still smiling to beat the band. "Pleasant dreams."

Chapter Four

Cedar spent the better part of Saturday washing clothes and cleaning her house from top to bottom. After completing those chores, she went shopping for groceries. She was, she knew, staying as busy as possible so she wouldn't dwell on the kiss she'd shared with Mark Chandler.

Her plan was to be so exhausted by the end of the day that she'd tumble into bed and fall instantly asleep instead of tossing and turning all night as she'd done after returning from Mark's the previous evening.

Her grand scheme was a total flop.

Saturday was an equally restless night that included dreams of Mark when she did manage to sleep. On Sunday morning, Cedar flung back the blankets on her bed and stomped into the bathroom only to shiver her way through a quick shower when she discovered she had no hot water.

After dressing in jeans, heavy socks and a bulky fisherman's sweater, she went to the laundry room and opened the door to the small enclosure where the water heater was housed to discover a puddle of water on the floor and a dead-as-a-doornail heater.

She returned to the kitchen and consumed a much-needed cup of coffee, after which she fed Oreo, then tossed the telephone book on the table to begin the phone marathon to find a business that would deliver and install a new water heater on a Sunday. Her efforts resulted in nothing more than endless recorded messages announcing Monday through Saturday business hours.

"House," Cedar said, narrowing her eyes, "I've really had it with you. This is it, the last straw."

She drummed her fingers on the table as she searched her mind for a solution. Her biggest concern was that the bottom of the heater would go and she would have a forty-gallon flood to deal with before she could get someone to the house the next day.

"Wait a minute," she said, sitting up straighter.

Mark Chandler was a bigwig in the construction arena. He no doubt knew suppliers of everything needed to complete a building or house. She would call Mark and ask him if—

"No," Cedar said. "Bad idea. Bad, bad, bad."

She was having enough difficulty dealing with Mark as a client without contacting him on a non-psychology matter.

Cedar went back into the laundry room and moaned aloud when she saw that the pool of water from the heater was now slowly seeping beneath the enclosure door. She mopped the floor, laid some old towels, then sighed.

Desperate times, she thought, required desperate measures. She would telephone Mark because she had no idea what else to do.

She returned to the kitchen table, flipped through the phone book again and punched in the numbers on the portable telephone before she lost her nerve. One ring, two rings…

"Hello?"

"Mark? This is Cedar. Cedar Kennedy."

"Good morning, Cedar Kennedy. You didn't have to identify yourself, because I recognized your voice."

"You did?" she said, unable to curb a smile.

"Fancy that." She shook her head slightly and cleared her throat. "I'm sorry to disturb you on a Sunday morning, and I'm not calling as Dr. Kennedy, just as me, Cedar. I have this problem, you see, and I've tried every company in the book and no one is working today, and I was hoping that you might, maybe, be able to—"

"Whoa," Mark interrupted. "You'd better stop and take a breath before you pass out from lack of oxygen. Slow down and start at the top. What's the problem you're referring to?"

Cedar plunked her elbow on the table and pressed her palm to her forehead as she explained to Mark what had happened, then asked if he knew someone who would be willing to help her.

"Okay, I understand the situation," he said. "Sit tight."

"I..." Cedar said, then realized she was talking to the dial tone.

Restless and edgy, Cedar went back upstairs, made her bed, then straightened the towels in the bathroom. She returned to the kitchen and ate a bagel, then paced around the living room, stopping only twice to check that the phone was still working.

Two hours after she had telephoned Mark, the doorbell rang, causing her to gasp and splay one hand over her racing heart. She opened the door to find Mark and Joey on her front porch.

"Hi," Mark said, then turned and motioned to someone out of Cedar's view. "Joey and I are going door to door selling forty-gallon water heaters. Want one?"

"Oh, thank you, thank you, thank you," Cedar said. "You're a miracle worker. I appreciate this so much, Mark. I—"

"Can I see your cat?" Joey asked.

"What?" Cedar said. "Oh, sure. Come in."

"Have you got a back door closer to where the heater is?" Mark said. "Moose has the new one off the truck, but it would be best not to push the dolly over your carpeting."

"Moose?" Cedar said.

"He's really, really big," Joey said, awe in his tone. "Like a giant, you know?"

Cedar peered around the door frame and her eyes widened.

"Heavens, you're right," she said. "But he's a very nice giant to do this on a Sunday."

"We're buddies," Mark said, smiling. "Rear door?"

"Through the kitchen door in the backyard."

"Got it," Mark said. "You keep an eye on Joey and leave the rest to Moose and me."

A few minutes later, Cedar was showing Moose, Mark and Joey the laundry room where the water heater was housed.

"The bottom of that baby is about to let go," Moose said, examining the patient. "Well, no sweat. We'll just switch it out with the new one I brought. Piece of cake."

"Thank you," Cedar said. "I mean it. Thank you so much and—"

"You're wearing out the thank-you thing," Mark said, laughing. "You're welcome. You and Joey get out of the way and…oh, hello, cat. You must be Oreo. You're gone, too. Joey, grab that cat."

Joey picked up Oreo who allowed the little boy to carry her to the living room. Cedar followed close behind and the trio settled onto the sofa.

"Cool cat," Joey said, stroking a purring Oreo, who was sprawled across his lap. "I wish I had a cat. Or a dog. Or something. A pet that was all mine."

"Well, Oreo certainly likes you, Joey," Cedar said, ruffling his hair. "I hope you didn't mind that I disturbed your morning."

"Nope," Joey said. "Uncle Mark said good guys always rescue damn cells in dress, whatever that means."

"I think he said damsels in distress," Cedar said, laughing. "That's a lady in trouble and I certainly qualify."

"Oh," Joey said, nodding. "Well, Uncle Mark said it was great to have a chance to help you 'cause you're helping us."

"That was a lovely thing for him to say," Cedar said, feeling what could only be described as warm fuzzies swish through her. "I'm very fortunate to have you and your Uncle Mark as friends."

"Yeah?" Joey said, his face lighting up as he looked at her.

"Yeah," Cedar said, smiling as she nodded.

Joey suddenly frowned. He switched his gaze back to Oreo and began to stroke her again.

"Friends are supposed to be forever," he said quietly. "There's lots of things that are supposed to be forever, but then they're not forever and…" He stopped speaking and shrugged.

"That doesn't mean you should stop believing in forever, Joey," Cedar said, sliding one arm across his shoulders. "Promises do get broken, but sometimes it's no one's fault."

Joey jerked sideways, making it clear that he wanted her to remove her arm. His sudden motion startled Oreo and the cat jumped off Joey's lap and ran from the room.

"Oreo," Cedar called. "Oreo, come back here. Come on, pretty girl. Joey wants to play with you."

"No, I don't," he said, dropping his chin to his

chest. "I don't care that she ran away because I don't like her anyway. She's just a dumb cat and her name is dumb, too. She's not a cookie, she's a dumb, stupid cat."

"You can feel that way if you want to," Cedar said gently, "but she's very special to me. If anything happened to Oreo, I would be so sad and I'd cry and cry. Oreo greets me when I come home and sits close by me in the evenings when I'm here alone. It's nice to know she wants to be with me, just like your Uncle Mark wants to be with you."

"He has to be with me because if he left me all alone in the house, the police would come and put him in jail," Joey said, glowering at Cedar. "Benny told me that people who leave little kids by themself get arrested and they throw away the key.

"Uncle Mark didn't even have a bed for me when I came 'cause he didn't want a kid so he left the rooms empty, but then he had to buy me a bed and stuff. I bet he's still mad about having to pay all that money so I had a bed and dresser and junk. If you ask him, I bet he'll tell you he's still mad about that."

"No, he is not," Cedar said firmly. "He wanted you to have a bedroom you are comfortable in, no matter what it cost. The money wasn't important to him, Joey, you are."

"He got me a Game Boy, but I left it in the box."

"Why?"

"'Cause I figure he'll change his mind and want to take it back to the store. He never said I could keep it forever, so…" Joey shrugged.

"Well, even if he said you could keep it forever, you probably wouldn't play with it. I mean, hey, you don't believe in forever anymore, remember?"

"I would about a Game Boy," Joey said quickly.

"Really?" Cedar said.

"Well, yeah," Joey said.

"You're all set, Cedar," Mark said, entering the living room with the enormous Moose.

"I put your old heater in my truck," Moose said. "You didn't want it, did you? To make into a planter or something?"

"No," Cedar said, laughing as she got to her feet.

Moose extended a clipboard toward her. "If you'll sign this, I'll mail it off to activate the guarantee," he said.

Cedar took the clipboard, looked at the bill and frowned. "This only lists the cost for the heater, Moose," she said. "You need to add your labor to this."

"Naw," he said, "not necessary. Mark says you're a special lady and that's good enough for me. Besides, he helped me build a dynamite deck on the back of my house in his free time last year and it's the envy of everybody on my block. I owe him one."

"But…" Cedar said.

"Sign the paper," Mark said. "Moose has to get home and clean out the gutters on his house or his wife will string him up by the thumbs. She's a scary woman…all five feet of her."

Moose chuckled. "You got that straight. I love her with all my heart, but I sure don't cross her."

"This is very generous of you," Cedar said, then signed the sheet.

"I like this house," Moose said, glancing around. "These old places have a lot of personality."

"I'm clashing with that personality," Cedar said, shaking her head. "I've done nothing but pour money into repairs and I've had enough. This monster is going on the market so I can get out of here."

Joey slid off the sofa and curled his hands into tight fists at his sides. "You're leaving?" he shouted. "You're selling your house and going away? What kind of friend is that? Not a forever friend. No way, no way, no way."

"Joey, stop it," Mark said. "Quit yelling at Cedar like that. It's very rude."

"Joey, listen to me," Cedar said, gripping his shoulders. "I'm just planning to move to another house in Phoenix. I'm not going away, never to be seen again. I made a mistake when I bought this place. I need a newer house where things don't break all the time. I'll still be your friend and you'll be mine. That is not going to change."

"Oh," Joey said in a small voice.

"How about an apology for shouting at Cedar?" Mark said.

"Sorry," Joey mumbled.

"I'll put the word out about this house," Moose said. "It won't be on the market long. Nice to meet you, Cedar. Catch you later, Mark. Joey, stay cool, dude."

"Thank you again, Moose," Cedar said, releasing her hold on Joey and smiling at the big man.

"My pleasure," Moose said. "I'll see myself out."

"Well," Cedar said, after Moose left the house, "the least I can do is fix some lunch for my heroes to the rescue. How does grilled cheese sandwiches and vegetable soup sound?"

"Aren't you mad at me 'cause I yelled at you?" Joey said, staring at the toes of his sneakers.

"No, Joey," Cedar said, "I'm not angry. You misunderstood what I meant about leaving. Perhaps I owe you an apology for not making it clear right away that I'm staying in Phoenix. I'm sorry."

"'Kay," Joey said, still not looking at her.

"It's a shame you can't keep this place," Mark said, glancing around, "but I can understand your position. If you're not able to do repairs yourself, you're living in a money pit."

Cedar laughed. "My father warned me about that, but I didn't listen because I was so enchanted with this house. Ugh, I'll have to suffer through his I-told-you-so routine. Serves me right, I suppose."

"Uncle Mark could fix all your stuff when it breaks," Joey said. "Then you could stay here like you want to and you won't have to be sad about leaving."

"I won't be sad, honey," Cedar said, smiling. "More like…oh, disappointed. Once I get over that, I'll start to get excited about having a newer place, all shiny and pretty and not falling apart. It's really best to look forward, Joey, not back. Understand?"

Joey shrugged.

Oreo strolled back into the living room.

"Oreo returns," Cedar said. "Joey, she has some toys in that little basket over there. Why don't you see if she'll play with you? I'll call you when lunch is ready."

"'Kay," Joey said. "Come on, Oreo. Know what? Cedar named you after a cookie. That is so lame, but I guess you don't care. Come on, let's play."

As if she'd understood every word Joey said, Oreo bounded across the room to the toy basket and tipped it over, dumping out the toys. Joey dropped to his knees and held up a string attached to a plastic ball with a bell inside. Oreo batted at the toy and Joey laughed.

"Joey is laughing," Mark whispered to Cedar. "He's actually playing and laughing."

"One point for the good guys," Cedar said, smiling. "Let's leave him alone so he doesn't feel as though he's under a microscope. You can watch me fix lunch."

In the kitchen, after they'd washed their hands, Mark volunteered to set the table while Cedar prepared the meal.

"Joey gets really panicked about anyone leaving, doesn't he?" Mark said, as he placed napkins on the table. "He went nuts when he thought you were going away."

"That's understandable, Mark," she said, dumping a can of soup in a pan. "He lost his parents. They went away. Leaving, to Joey, means you don't come back. He's very fragile in so many areas. I can't begin to work through those things with him until he gives way to the emotions he's holding in such tight check. He needs to cry. Dear heaven, how that sweet little boy needs to cry."

Mark moved behind Cedar where she stood at the stove and placed his hands on her shoulders.

"You really care about Joey, don't you?" he said. "About all the kids you try to help, I imagine. Doesn't that drain you?"

"Sometimes," she said, attempting and failing

to ignore the warmth that spread throughout her from Mark's touch. "I often wish I had a magic wand that I could wave to solve all their problems. But all I can do is my best and hope it's enough."

"I'm very glad I found you," Mark said, then cleared his throat. "For Joey." He dropped his hands from her shoulders and stepped back. "What…what else can I do to help with lunch?"

"Oh…get some glasses out of the cupboard."

"Yes, ma'am."

It seemed to Cedar as if everything was moving in slow motion. The soup wouldn't heat quickly enough, the cheese was taking forever to melt on the sandwiches, the ice cubes refused to pop out of the plastic trays. As time dragged while she tried to get the simple meal on the table, the tension between her and Mark built, virtually crackling in the air. Whenever they caught each other's gaze, they looked quickly away and busied themselves with some task. Mark spilled the milk he was pouring for Joey. Cedar forgot the soup and it boiled over the top of the pan.

"Oh, for crying out loud," she said, plunking the pan on another burner. "This is ridiculous."

"No, it's not," Mark said. "I'm not certain what it is, but it's definitely not ridiculous. You push buttons I didn't even know I had, Cedar. Nothing like this has happened to me before. Don't you want to know what this is?"

"No," she said, turning from the stove to look at him. "No, I don't." She sighed. "Mark, just concentrate on Joey. He needs every spare second you have to be focused on him and what he's going through.

"I'd like to see you cut back on your work hours so you can spend more time with him and… You have no room in your life for *anything* else than what you're dealing with now. And I don't, either. That is that. End of story. Okay?"

Mark executed such a perfect rendition of one of Joey's shrugs that Cedar couldn't help but burst into laughter, which finally dispelled the tension in the kitchen.

"That shrug," she said, shaking her head. "Between you and Joey, I'll probably end up having nightmares about it. Enough of this. Let's get this meal, such as it is, on the table. I consider myself a decent cook, but not today. Would you tell Joey to wash his hands, please?"

They consumed their lunch with Joey talking animatedly about Oreo's antics with the toys. Afterward, Cedar declined Mark's offer to help clean up, explaining that she had work to do and would see them at their appointment at her office the next afternoon. She thanked Mark again for coming to her rescue as she walked the pair to the front door.

"Is this the bum's rush?" Mark said.

"The what?" Joey said.

"No, no, of course not," Cedar said. "I have things I need to do, that's all."

"Can I come see Oreo again?" Joey said.

"Sure," Cedar said. "We'll schedule something, Joey. I'm certain she'll be very pleased to see you because I don't have as much time to play with her as I used to. Mark, you will think about cutting back on your work hours, won't you?"

"I don't believe that's possible, but…yeah, I'll think about it. I have a lot of irons in the fire, Cedar. My company is growing bigger all the time with all the jobs I'm getting."

"Just how big does it have to get?" Cedar said.

"As I've said before, I have certain goals," Mark said.

"Things change, Mark."

"And some things don't."

"Well, we'll get into that another time," Cedar said. "By the way, do you plan to take the Game Boy you gave Joey back to the store?"

"No, of course not," Mark said, obviously confused.

"So Joey can keep it forever?" Cedar said.

"Oh, I see," Mark said, nodding slowly. "Joey, the Game Boy is yours forever. You can leave it in the box, play with it, whatever suits you. It's none of my business because it belongs to you."

"Really?" Joey said. "Forever?"

"Forever," Mark said, nodding.

"Way cool," Joey said. "I'm going to play with it today."

"Good," Cedar said. "Well, goodbye for today, my friend, Joey. I'll see you tomorrow."

"I'm looking forward to it," Mark said, producing his best one-hundred-watt smile.

"'Bye," Joey said. "'Bye, Oreo."

Cedar closed the door, leaned against it and closed her eyes for a long moment before heading back to the kitchen to clean up.

"Mark Chandler," she said, stomping across the living room, "you are driving me nuts, mister, and I don't like it. Not one little bit."

In the late afternoon, Mark stood in the doorway of Joey's bedroom and watched the little boy concentrating on mastering the Game Boy as he lay on his bed. Mark smiled, then wandered back to the living room.

He had some blueprints he should be looking over, but he just wasn't in the mood, which was unusual for him. Ordinarily, if something needed to be done for Chandler Construction, he did it with no hesitation or second thoughts.

But his thoughts were the problem. Thoughts of Cedar. When he'd placed his hands on her shoulders while she stood at the stove, it had taken every bit of willpower he possessed to keep from turning her around, pulling her close and kissing her until neither of them could breathe. That image was haunting him now.

Mark slouched into his favorite chair, propped his elbows on the arms, made a steeple of his fingers and tapped them against his lips.

There *was* something special happening between him and Cedar, and for reasons he couldn't get a handle on, he wanted to know what it all meant. That made no sense whatsoever because he had neither the time nor the intention of getting seriously involved at this point in his life.

Things change, Mark.

Damn it, there he went again, chasing his confused thoughts around in his mind like a gerbil on one of those never-ending trips on a wheel that got the poor critter nowhere.

Still, Cedar had acknowledged that something was happening between them, but she had been lightning-fast to make clear she wasn't interested in exploring what that something might be. She sure knew how to slice and dice a guy's ego, for Pete's sake. He wasn't a man, he was a client. Hell.

Take a break, brain, Mark directed, then picked up the remote and found a football game to watch on television.

When the portable telephone he'd left on the table next to his chair rang, Mark jerked awake. He glanced at his watch, saw that he'd slept for about half an hour, then snatched up the phone.

"Yeah?" He yawned. "Hello?"

"Mark? It's Cedar. I'm sorry to disturb you at home again, but…did I wake you?"

"I guess so," he said. "I thought I was watching football. What's up? Did something else break? Do you need a stove, refrigerator, or a—"

"Heavens, don't even joke about such things," she said, laughing. "I have enough problems with this monster of a house as it is." She paused. "I was just reviewing my schedule for the week and wanted you to know now that I'm canceling Joey's appointment for Wednesday, so you don't have to take off work early that day."

Mark sat up straighter in the chair.

"Why don't you want to see me…us…him on Wednesday?"

"Because we were together Friday and again

today and you're coming in tomorrow. Joey needs a breather, time to think the issues we discuss without hearing everything repeated so soon. I don't want him to get to the point where he's tuning me out with a been-here, heard-this attitude."

"Oh," Mark said. "Well, yeah, I guess that makes sense. Hey, Joey has been playing with the Game Boy all afternoon. He's flopped on his bed like a regular little kid having a good time."

"Oh, I'm so pleased to hear that. *You* made that happen by letting him know the toy was his forever. In Joey's mind, the thought of believing in forever is terrifying, given the loss he's suffered. Foremost, he needs to be assured that he can live with you forever, no matter what he does. Oh, and if the opportunity presents itself, you should let him know you didn't mind one bit spending the money for his bedroom furniture."

"He's worried about *that?*"

"Mark, at this point in time our little guy is worried about a long, long list of things."

"*Our* little guy?"

"Well, yes. I mean, we're working together to help him be the happy child he deserves to be."

"You. Me. Together. Interesting."

"Mark, please, don't twist what I'm saying into…just don't."

"Well, try this on for size, Dr. Kennedy," Mark said, narrowing his eyes. "You said I should cut back on *my* work load hours, but *you* sure put in twenty-four/seven for your career. We could both use a break, right? What if I got a sitter for Joey and you and I go out to dinner?

"It's a win-win proposition. Joey gets time off from dealing with his Uncle Mark to interact with someone new and you and I take a practice run at not thinking about our careers. That's good mental health all the way around the block."

"Yes, it is, but I don't think—"

"You wouldn't be going out with a client, because we wouldn't talk about Joey. We'd just be two people enjoying each other's company and attempting to achieve a better work-and-play balance in their lives. How's that? Pretty good shrinky-dink stuff, huh?"

Cedar laughed. "I think you could sell refrigerators to Eskimos."

"Dinner? Wednesday night? I'll pick you up at seven o'clock. Say yes, Cedar."

One silent second passed, then two, then three. Mark's hold on the telephone tightened.

Until he heard Cedar's softly spoken answer.

"Yes."

Chapter Five

On Monday afternoon, Cedar sat in her office sipping a hot cup of tea as she stared into space. She'd spent the morning at a day-care center observing a four-year-old client who was in foster care because her parents were in jail for selling drugs. Rosie was angry and scared, and was extremely aggressive around other children, often pushing them away or grabbing their toys. Cedar shook her head as she recalled what she had seen.

Rosie had been enrolled in day-care at Cedar's suggestion to determine the child's social skills. But from what Cedar had witnessed it was very obvious that Rosie was not ready for daily contact with other kids. She needed to stay at home and have some quiet one-on-one time with her foster mother until she calmed down and began to adjust to her new environment. Undivided attention was possible as the other foster children were in school. The life she had known had been horrendous, but it was familiar and hers. Rosie needed time and lots and lots of hugs.

Cedar sighed and finished her tea.

She certainly was proficient at figuring out why her clients acted as they did, she thought dryly. Wouldn't it be nice if she knew why *she* had agreed to go out to dinner with Mark Chandler? The answer to that question would be most welcome and might allow her to get a decent night's sleep.

She felt as though she was split in two. Two Cedars. The purely professional Cedar was furious at herself for breaking her rule of never socializing with her clients. The other Cedar, the purely feminine one, was looking forward to her evening with Mark so much, it was borderline ridiculous.

It had been too long since she'd just enjoyed herself. She'd been putting in long hours at work for weeks, months, plus dealing with her dud of a house, so Mark's invitation had caught her at a time when she was tired and vulnerable. The idea of wearing a pretty dress and being pampered for a few hours had sounded heavenly.

If she stopped right there with her rationale for accepting Mark's invitation, she'd be copping out. She knew darn well that she'd broken her own rule because Mark the man had tempted her to do so.

Enough of this. She was driving herself nuts thinking about Wednesday night at seven o'clock. She was simply going out to dinner with a very handsome man and she intended to have a wonderful evening. The earth wouldn't stop turning because she'd decided to spend a few hours feeling pretty and womanly.

The intercom on Cedar's desk buzzed and she jerked slightly at the sudden interruption before pressing the button on the box.

"Yes, Bethany?"

"Cindy is here," Bethany said.

"Have her come in."

Cedar got to her feet as Cindy entered the office. The girl stomped across the room and sat down, a stormy expression on her face.

"Hello, Cindy," Cedar said, settling back into her chair. "How are you?"

"You would not believe how much apartments cost," Cindy said. "Real slummy dumps, too. They rip people off so bad it's a crime. It's, like, so unfair.

And guess what else? I can't even get a job because I'm only fifteen. Is that bogus or what?

"Some fast-food places said to come back when I was sixteen but they didn't act real thrilled that I was pregnant and said they'd want to know what arrangements I'd made for my baby's care so they could be sure I'd show up for work. And day care? Forget day care. They charge so much you'd think they were feeding those kids with silver spoons or something. I just…I just…"

Cindy burst into tears.

"I just don't know what I'm going to do," she wailed.

Cedar offered Cindy a tissue from the box she kept on the corner of her desk. Cindy yanked a few tissues free and dabbed at her nose.

"I'm tired of being pregnant, too." She sniffled.

"You're only about six and a half months along, Cindy," Cedar said. "You have a ways to go, you know."

"Yeah, I know, but I'm fat and bored and this kid clobbers me all the time, and…this is my mother's fault. If she didn't kick me out, I could have my baby and live at home and—"

"Whoa," Cedar said, raising one hand. "Your mother had nothing to do with your getting pregnant. That was your doing. I respect your mother for knowing she had enough on her plate with your brothers and sisters without adding an infant. Putting you in foster care wasn't an easy decision for her to make, but she did what she felt was best for everyone. You can't expect your mother to raise your baby."

"But—"

"Cindy, have you given any more thought to finishing high school? You were offered a traveling teacher from your school district who would come to your foster home and get you to the point where you could take the GED test, but you refused. You also dropped out of the classes provided for pregnant teens at your school because you said you felt like a freak on display crossing the campus. Now you say that you're bored. Why not work toward your GED?"

"Yeah, I suppose. I might be able to get a better job than a fast-food thing."

"Mmm," Cedar said, nodding.

"But a GED isn't going to make it possible for me to have enough money for a decent apartment and day care and…I went over to my friend's house and she showed me her dress for the Christmas dance, you know? The school rented this ballroom at a fancy hotel, you know? Her boyfriend is going to wear a tux, a real tux with a red cummerbund to match her dress and…"

Two tears slid down Cindy's cheeks.

"I want to go to that dance," she said. "I'm never going to have a fancy dress or go to another dance for as long as I live. Never. Oh, God, what am I going to do? I want my baby, I swear I do, but…but the thing is, I'll be a mother, you know? I'm just a kid who wants to go to the Christmas dance and…" Cindy covered her face with her hands.

"Honey," Cedar said gently, "mothers don't have time to go to high-school dances."

"I…know." Cindy dropped her hands to splay over her stomach. "I can't do this. I can't, Cedar. I was so happy about this baby…it's a girl, did I tell you that?…I was so happy that she was going to be mine, to love me no matter what, and I thought I'd have a nice apartment with a nursery with bunny wallpaper, and a bunch of cute clothes for my baby. My friends would be so envious because I was so grown up and they were still dragging off to school everyday and…when my friend showed me her dress for the dance, she said she felt so sorry for me, and I felt so sorry for me, too."

"Do you see a solution to all of this, Cindy?" Cedar said.

"No. Yes. I mean, maybe I should think—just think—a little about letting someone adopt my baby. Maybe. Someone who could give her cute clothes and a nice nursery with bunny wallpaper and…but she's mine, Cedar. But I can't…I can't give her anything."

"Well, you don't have to make a final decision at this point," Cedar said. "What you could do is have your CPS social worker show you some applications from people who want to adopt. You'll see a picture of them, of their home, learn about them and what they could offer your baby. Looking doesn't obligate you to anything. What do you think?"

"I guess I could do that. Maybe. Maybe not. I don't know. Yeah, I guess I could look at the applications, huh? But I was thinking, Cedar, that…that *you* might adopt my baby. I mean, if I decided to let someone adopt her, I'd want you because you're so nice and you're old, you know, not a kid like me, and I know shrinks make lots of money so you could buy the cute clothes and—"

"Cindy, stop," Cedar interrupted. "I'm a single woman. You'd want to pick a couple, a mother and father, for the baby."

"Why? My dad split years ago and my mom does a super job all on her own. We don't have much money, but everybody is happy and…I want to go home to my mom and my brothers and sisters, and go back to school so I can go to dances and wear pretty dresses. I do, Cedar.

"If you had my baby, I'd know for sure she was okay, and I wouldn't bother you or ask to visit her or anything like that. I promise I wouldn't. I'd even sign a paper to say I'd never bug you or show up at your house."

"Cindy, please, calm down. Let's go back to your looking at applications from couples, all right? I'll contact your social worker and she'll make an appointment with you to review some applications."

"Don't you want to be a mother?" Cindy said.

Yes, Cedar's mind yelled. Oh, Cindy, you have no idea how much I want to be a mother, but— Don't do this to me, darling girl. You're breaking my heart.

"That's not what we're discussing," Cedar said, hearing the slight quiver in her voice as she stood. "Honey, our time is up. Your social worker will be in touch, and next week you can tell me what you thought of the couples you read about. Would you like to meet in a pretty park?"

"No, I like it here because it's private." Cindy got to her feet. "Will you think about taking my baby?"

"I…"

"Please, Cedar? Just say you'll think about it?"

"I…well…"

"Good. 'Bye."

Cindy hurried from the room and Cedar sank back into her chair, totally drained.

She hadn't handled that well at all, she fumed, pressing her fingertips to her painfully throbbing temples. She never should have allowed Cindy to leave believing that she was actually considering adopting her baby. She should have made it perfectly clear that no, she would not give it further thought because it was out of the question.

Cedar sighed.

A baby. A precious baby girl. She'd hesitated instead of making certain that Cindy knew her offer could not be considered. Hesitated, because for that tick of time she could literally feel that tiny bundle being placed in her arms and that cold, empty place within herself fill with warmth and love and—

"Oh, God," Cedar said, as tears filled her eyes. "Stop it. Cindy caught you off guard, but that's no excuse for thinking even for a second that…no. No, no, no. And next week I'll be certain that Cindy understands that. I will. Yes, I will."

The intercom buzzed and Cedar pressed the button with a finger that was not quite steady.

"Yes, Bethany?"

"Joey is here."

And Mark, Cedar thought, closing her eyes for a moment. What if he saw, sensed, that she was upset and asked her what was wrong? No, she mustn't allow that to happen.

"Give me a minute, Bethany. I'll buzz you when I'm ready to see Joey."

"Okey-dokey. He's having his snack now anyway."

Cedar got to her feet and went into the small bathroom at the rear of the office. Inside, she gripped the sink and leaned forward to scrutinize her reflection to determine if there was any evidence that she had been shaken to the depths of her soul, the painful memories still hovering like beasts in the shadows eager to attack.

She was rather pale, she decided, but if Mark commented on her pasty complexion, she'd simply say that she'd had a busy day and was weary. She'd lie like Pinocchio and give Joey a thrill because he could watch her nose grow.

"You're getting hysterical," Cedar told her image in the mirror. "Cindy gave you a wonderful compliment by suggesting that you adopt her baby girl and you're acting like she beat you up. Get a grip."

Cedar straightened, squared her shoulders and left the bathroom. She hesitated at her desk, then decided to act like the professional that she was by getting Joey herself and even smiling nicely at Mark.

When she opened the door and stepped into the outer office, she stopped at the sight of a strange man sitting with Joey on the sofa.

"Hello, Joey," she said.

"Hi," he said, then made a loud slurping noise as he drained his juice box.

The man beside him got to his feet.

"Hi," he said. "I'm Jeff Mason. I work for Mark. One of our guys got hurt on the job and Mark went to the hospital with him. He always does that, sticks right with the guy until he knows everything is all right. A lot of bosses wouldn't do that, but Mark…anyway, I picked up Joey and brought him over here and I'll keep him with me when you're done until Mark calls me on my cell and tells me where to take the kiddo. If it gets late, I can take Joey home because Mark gave me the key to his house."

"Oh, I see," Cedar said after the man had finished talking. That was not disappointment she was feeling because Mark wasn't there, was it? No, it wasn't. Yes, it was. She might as well admit it and top off this lousy day she was having in style. "That's fine. Joey, are you ready to have a little chat?"

"No," Joey said, pressing himself deeper into the sofa. "I don't want to talk today. No."

"Okay, no problem. Just come into my office and sit with me and we'll stare at each other."

"That's dumb," Joey said.

"Hey," Jeff said, "you're being kinda rude there,

Joey. I don't think your Uncle Mark will want to hear that you were rude when we got here. Go."

Joey executed one of his dramatic shrugs, slid off the sofa and shuffled past Cedar, dragging his feet through the carpet.

"Aren't kids a kick?" Jeff said, smiling at Cedar. "I have four myself and I think they're a hoot."

A thrill a minute, Cedar thought as she produced a smile for Jeff's benefit.

The session with Joey did not go well. He was sullen and unresponsive, the only bright spot coming when he told her that his Uncle Mark had learned how to make pancakes that were sorta gross but not as gross as the scrambled eggs.

Part of the problem, Cedar knew, was that she was not on top of her game, so to speak. She prided herself on her expertise at getting recalcitrant clients to reveal at least some clue as to where they were emotionally during a particular session, but today she was failing miserably with sad and angry little Joey.

"Well, my friend," Cedar said finally, "I think we'll cut this a bit short today." She paused. "Joey, do you feel all right?"

"My head hurts," he said, frowning. "My stomach hurts. And my feet hurt. My hair doesn't feel too great, either. Maybe Uncle Mark poisoned me with them pancakes."

"That's possible, I suppose," Cedar said, getting to her feet, "but if he did, he didn't mean to." She walked over to Joey and placed one hand on his forehead. "You're a tad warm. Maybe you're getting a bug."

Joey's eyes widened. "Like head lice?"

"No," Cedar said, smiling. "I mean, you just aren't feeling up to par, that's all. Why don't I have Jeff take you home?"

Joey shrugged.

In the reception area Cedar explained to Jeff that Joey needed some baby aspirin, a light dinner and should be tucked into bed early.

"I'm not a baby," Joey yelled. "Why are you telling him to give me baby stuff?"

"Correct that, Jeff," Cedar said. "I meant to say the kind of aspirin that is given to brave young boys who aren't quite old enough for adult aspirin. Are you with me, Mr. Father of Four?"

"Got it," Jeff said, chuckling. "Don't worry about a thing."

"Thank you," Cedar said. "It was nice to meet you, Jeff. I hope the injured member of your crew is going to be all right. Goodbye for now, Joey."

"'Bye," Joey mumbled.

After the pair left the office, Cedar turned to Bethany. "I am going home, taking four adult aspirin, having a light supper, and tucking *myself* into bed, and I don't intend to emerge for the next five years."

Bethany was still laughing when Cedar made her escape.

Chapter Six

On Wednesday evening, Mark stood in front of the bathroom mirror and worked on creating a decent knot in his tie. Joey watched him intently from his perch on the edge of the tub.

"A woman invented ties," Mark said, "to torture men. Trust me, no guy would do this to another guy."

Joey giggled and Mark smiled at the sound he so rarely heard coming from his nephew.

Should he ask Joey if he'd ever watched his father struggle with a tie? Mark wondered. No, he'd better not. He didn't want to do anything to destroy this moment. Joey had actually wandered in here on his own, instead of hiding in his room as was his usual routine.

"Are you and Cedar going to eat fancy food at a fancy restaurant?" Joey asked.

"She can have fancy if she wants to," Mark said, yanking the tie free and starting over. "Me? I'm going for a big juicy steak. That's not very nice of me, huh? Considering that I served you macaroni and cheese my crew could use to seal bricks together?"

Joey shrugged. "It was just medium gross, not totally gross. Do you think Cedar will wear a pretty dress tonight?"

"Sure. But I think she looks pretty in anything she wears."

"Yeah. You like Cedar a lot, don't you, Uncle Mark?"

"How much is a lot?" Mark said.

"Well, you know, you might, you know…kiss her."

Mark snapped his head around to stare at Joey. "*Kiss* her? Aren't you a bit young to be thinking about kissing?"

"Everybody knows about kissing," Joey said, frowning. "Geez. The next time I see Cedar, I'm going to ask her if you kissed her."

"No, you are not," Mark said, pointing a finger at Joey. "That's a question you don't ask. Kissing is a private thing and you don't go around doing a survey on who is kissing who. Or whom. Or whatever. If I kiss Cedar, it will be nobody's business but ours."

"You're going to kiss her," Joey said, nodding. "I can tell 'cause you're getting all grumpy about it and stuff to be sure I don't ask her if you did."

"Knock it off," Mark said, redirecting his attention to the mirror and fixing the tie.

"It will be good if you kiss Cedar because she's cool and I like her," Joey said. "She asks me too much stuff sometimes, but she's still cool and she smells good. Like a girl. Not a sweaty girl. A girl who just took a bath."

Mark chuckled.

"Maybe you could kiss her," Joey continued, "and make her smile at you real nice and stuff, then ask her if she wants to live with us."

"I beg your pardon?"

"Well, Cedar's house is falling down and she needs to get another one and there's room for her here. She cooks good and when we all eat together it's fun and there's talking and stuff instead of just eating and getting done. And you like her and I like her, and I like her cat, and I think Cedar likes us okay, so…."

The doorbell rang and Mark looked heavenward in gratitude that he had been saved from having to address Joey's dissertation.

"There's Sally, your sitter. She said she'd walk over since she only lives across the street," Mark said. "She's a senior in high school and babysits a lot so you should have some fun with her."

The doorbell chimed again.

"Go answer the door, Joey, before she thinks we skipped town."

"'Kay."

As Joey ran from the bathroom, Mark smoothed the tie down the front of his shirt. "That's as good as it gets," he said, then went into his bedroom to retrieve his suit jacket. Shrugging into the jacket, he glanced around the large, nicely furnished room.

Ask her if she wants to live with us.

Boy, oh, boy, when Joey came out from behind his walls for a visit, he sure talked up a storm. He had him kissing Cedar Kennedy, then moving her right in here so things could be fun.

Interesting proposition.

Mark started toward the door, then stopped and glanced back at the bed.

Imagine what it would be like to wake up each morning next to Cedar, he mused. A morning that followed a night of lovemaking so incredibly beautiful it defied description. She'd smile that sunshine smile of hers, add a dose of her wind-chime laughter, and make him glad to be alive and ready to start a new day.

And he would no longer be lonely.

"No longer…what?" Mark said aloud, planting his hands on his hips and scowling.

Where was this *lonely* notion coming from? he fumed. He didn't have time to be lonely. He was on a mission to achieve financial security, one he had mapped out years before. When he reached that goal, somewhere down the line, then and only then would he entertain the idea of having a wife and children and—

Well, he already had Joey and that was fine, great, would be even better once the little guy dealt with the pain of losing his parents. They'd be a team, doing father-and-son things together, like tossing a baseball around, going on hikes, cooking dinner with Cedar and—

"Uncle Mark," Joey said, running into the room, "Sally brought a thingy of popcorn to do in the microwave and said to ask you if it was okay if we did that."

"Oh, yeah, sure," Mark said. "You can have your snack with Sally."

Before he left, Mark gave the teenager instructions regarding Joey's bedtime and what he was allowed to watch on television.

"I don't know what time I'll be back, Sally," Mark said.

"No rush," Sally said. "I can always zonk out on the sofa if I get sleepy. Have a nice evening, Mr. Chandler."

"Don't forget to kiss Cedar," Joey said.

"I'm outta here," Mark said, as Sally burst into laughter.

Cedar slowly turned around in front of the full-length mirror on her closet door. When in doubt, she thought, wear the ever-famous little black dress, hers being wool crepe with long sleeves, a narrow belt and jewel neckline. She'd added a gold heart-shaped locket and small gold earrings, and her shoes were regulation two-inch black heels.

"And that," Cedar said, leaving the bedroom, "as they say, is that."

She decided to ignore the other addition to her ensemble, which was a bevy of butterflies that had arrived uninvited in her stomach. She was nervous, darn it, and that fact was infuriating. She was determined to set aside the butterflies and all thoughts of work and her crumbling house, and simply have a lovely evening in the company of a handsome man.

Cedar smiled. She could do this.

The doorbell rang.

She was still smiling when she opened the front door to Mark, but her smile faltered a tad as she drank in the sight of him in a charcoal-gray suit, dark-blue shirt and gray tie.

The man was beyond handsome, she thought.

"Hello, Cedar," Mark said, as he stepped into the living room. "You look sensational."

"Thank you," she said, closing the door. "So do you." She paused. "Would you care for something to drink?"

"I made reservations, so we really should get going," he said, then frowned. "Cedar, I just want to say that I've really been looking forward to this evening. I don't know why it's suddenly so important that I tell you that, but it is."

"What a nice thing to say, Mark. I…well. I've been looking forward to it, too."

"Good," he said, gazing into her eyes. "That's very, very good to hear."

They stood about two feet apart, not moving, hardly breathing, mesmerized by eyes of blue and fathomless depths of dark, dark eyes. The room around them faded into a hazy mist and the only sound they heard was the thundering of their own hearts echoing in their ears.

Heat began to swirl within them, fanning flames of desire that threatened to consume them.

Mark finally tore his gaze from hers and drew a rough breath.

"We…" he started, then cleared his throat. "We'd better go."

"What?" Cedar said dreamily, then blinked. "Oh. Yes, of course. I'll just get my purse and shawl, except I don't remember where I put them…there they are." She hurried to snatch them from a chair. "I'm ready."

Mark looked at her for a long moment before he spoke again.

"So am I," he said quietly.

A shiver slithered down Cedar's spine.

They left the house, but the heightened awareness, the hum of sexuality, the simmering heat accompanied them, taking greater hold as they drove across town, then found themselves, somehow, being seated at a table for two in one of Phoenix's finest restaurants.

They ordered from flocked menus, Mark tasted and approved a rich wine, then salads appeared before them.

"How is that member of your crew who was injured?" Cedar said, hoping her voice was steadier than it sounded to her.

"He'll be okay," Mark said, "but he's out of commission for now because he broke his wrist. He slipped going up a ladder, put out his hand to catch himself as he fell and snapped a bone."

"Oh, that's a shame," she said. "That Jeff who brought Joey to my office was very impressed with the fact that you always accompany an injured worker to the emergency room."

"It doesn't happen that often," Mark said, "but, yes, I tag along and see what's what."

"Joey wasn't feeling well when I saw him. Is he all right now?"

"He was fine by the next morning," Mark said. "Cedar, let's not talk about Joey tonight. Remember?"

"I remember. I don't want to discuss any of my clients, cold-hearted person that I am, nor my stressing-me-to-the-max house." Cedar took a bite of the crisp salad. "Mmm. Delicious. Mark, I'd like to hear about where you grew up. Were you always interested in construction? You know, creating things from odds and ends when you were little?"

"We…um…we moved around a lot," Mark said, looking at his salad, then pushing it aside. "There was never extra money for movies, or special outings, so, yes, I entertained myself by building junky things from whatever I could find. The majority of the time my sister…Mary…had to ask me what it was when I announced that my project was finished."

"You were that talented, huh?" Cedar said, smiling.

"It was grim, very grim, but I had fun doing it," he said. "Little by little, I got the hang of it and as I got older I knew that I wanted to have a career where I could create things that would be on this earth long after I was gone. I still get a rush from the process of starting with nothing, seeing a structure take shape, then seeing it completed."

"That must be very fulfilling," Cedar said, "to see and touch your creation. My work is more nebulous. I take a client as far as I'm capable, then hope that the positive changes I've witnessed stay in place in the future." She paused. "I promised myself I wouldn't talk about my career. Not tonight. I'd love to hear about something you made when you were, oh, say, Joey's age."

Mark laughed. "That's a long time ago. Give me a minute to trip down memory lane and come up with an example."

Just then the waiter appeared and placed their dinners in front of them. Mark had ordered a big steak that came with an enormous baked potato and mixed vegetables. Cedar had chosen baked salmon with dill sauce and steamed asparagus. They each sampled their meals, and agreed that everything was delicious.

"Sure beats Uncle Mark's scrambled eggs," Mark said, then took another bite of juicy steak.

"No offense, sir," Cedar said, laughing, "but rumor has it that just about *anything* beats Uncle Mark's scrambled eggs."

"True, very true," Mark said, nodding. "If it wasn't for you, I'd still be serving them to my nephew, the victim of my culinary arts. But, hey, now I know how to make barbecue chicken."

"Yes, you do. We need to expand your talents a bit further, though." Cedar paused. "You were going to tell me about something you made when you were little."

"Ah, yes, let me see," Mark said. "I made my mom a birdhouse one year for Mother's Day. I was about Joey's age, I guess. I hammered and glued and used duct tape to get that thing together, then painted it about ten different colors in stripes and circles. Man, that was one ugly birdhouse, but I was so proud of it, I was bursting my buttons."

Cedar made no attempt to hide her smile as she listened to Mark, envisioning the eager child working so hard on his precious gift for his mother. What a sweet and tender picture that created in her mind.

"The thing was," Mark went on, laughing softly,

"I forgot to make an opening so the birds could go inside the house."

"Oh, my," Cedar said.

"My mom was great. She said she was going to hang it from the tree anyway as a decoration that she could enjoy when she looked out the window as she washed dishes. It was so beautiful, she said, that it would make a chore like dishes a pleasure. My mom was…well, she was the best."

"I take it she's no longer living," Cedar said. "You didn't list any other relatives on the information sheet you filled out."

"My mother died when I was twenty. She died before I could…well, that's another story. Anyway, you have just heard the saga of the disastrous birdhouse created by Mark Chandler who, thank goodness, has a bit more expertise in the construction business now."

"More than a bit, I'd say," Cedar said. "Thank you for sharing the story about the birdhouse. You know, it might be a good thing for you and Joey to build something together."

"Joey who?" Mark said.

"Oops. I broke the rules again. No client talk. It's difficult, though, because Joey is such a big part of your life."

Mark remained silent, willing her, it seemed to stick to the rules.

Cedar shifted her attention to a safe place, her dinner.

As she ate, she thought about what Mark had started to tell about his mother. It sounded as if he had wanted to do something for her, but she had passed away before he could accomplish it. What had he been referring to? His quick change of subject and tone of voice had made clear she shouldn't push for details.

And what about his father? He had never once mentioned the man. He apparently was no longer living, either, because Mark hadn't listed him on the information sheet. Had his father been there when Mark made the birdhouse? When his mother had died? Why hadn't Mark made even one reference to his father?

"Cedar?"

"What? Oh, I'm sorry, I was woolgathering."

"The waiter is headed this way with the dessert trolley. Are you game?"

"I don't think I have room for..." Cedar stopped speaking as the waiter arrived at their table with the two-tier glass-shelf cart laden with scrumptious desserts. "Erase that. I'll find room. Oh, look at those creations. I hardly know which one to pick."

"I'll have Black Forest cake," Mark said.

"Yes, sir," the waiter said, placing a plate with a huge slice of the gooey delight on the table. "Madam?"

"Oh, maybe not," Cedar said. "The servings are all so large."

"Why don't we share this cake?" Mark said.

"Well, I guess…"

"Certainly, sir," the waiter said, placing another fork on the table. "Coffee?"

"Yes, please," Cedar and Mark said in unison.

Coffee arrived and the chocolate cake with the cherries dribbling down the sides was set in the center of the table.

Was there something rather…intimate about two people sharing one piece of cake? Cedar thought, picking up a fork. No, that was silly.

"Dig in," Mark said, then took a bite of cake at the same moment she swallowed hers.

"I…I think I've had enough cake," Cedar said, her voice trembling slightly, as she straightened in her chair. "It's sinfully delicious, but…oh, I refuse to play games. There's just something rather… rather…"

"Sensual about sharing a piece of cake?" Mark said.

"I'm being ridiculous," Cedar said, fiddling with her napkin.

"If you are, then you have company, because it's having the same effect on me, Cedar."

Cedar looked up slowly to meet Mark's gaze. "It is?"

"Oh, yeah," he said, placing his fork on the side of the plate. "Oh-h-h, yeah. Whew."

Cedar opened her mouth to reply, then realized she didn't have a clue what to say. She just sat there, hoping that Mark wasn't noticing the flush she felt warming her cheeks.

"Your cheeks have turned a pretty pink," he said.

So much for that hope, Cedar thought.

"That," Mark said, pointing one finger at the dessert, "is one very potent piece of cake."

In spite of her flustered state, Cedar laughed. "I think we're back to being ridiculous," she said.

"No, Cedar, there's nothing ridiculous about it," Mark said, suddenly serious. "We both felt the heat sizzling between us the minute I walked into your house tonight."

"I…"

"You said you refuse to play games," Mark continued, "and that's really great to hear, because I don't play games, either. You've felt what I have all evening, haven't you?"

"Yes," Cedar whispered.

"The question is, what are we going to do about it?" Mark said, his voice very deep and rumbly.

"I'd rather not discuss this…" Cedar glanced around. "…here."

"You're right. Shall we go?"

Cedar nodded and Mark signaled to the waiter for the check.

The drive to Cedar's house was made in total silence.

In her living room Cedar went through the motions of offering Mark something to drink, which he declined. With a sigh she sank into an easy chair as Mark settled on the sofa.

"I can't deny that I'm very attracted to you, Mark," Cedar finally said. "That's evident by the fact that I broke my own rule about never seeing a client socially. And, yes, I'm very aware that something extremely intense is happening between us. What it is, I don't know, but it can't be ignored."

"I agree."

"The thing is, I really have nothing to offer you. I have no intention of becoming involved in a serious relationship that might eventually lead to something permanent…like…like marriage. But since I met you, I've realized that I've been focusing entirely on my career. That's fulfilled me for a long time, but now…well, while my success has grown beyond my wildest hopes, I've become rather lonely.

"You make me feel special, Mark. I feel more alive and complete and…I desire you, I won't deny that. But if we make love, it would be an affair with no promises, no commitment to a future together."

"I understand," Mark said quietly. "I'm not in a position to commit to a permanent relationship, either, Cedar. I'm a long way from accomplishing what I've set out to do, and I won't be pulled from that path.

"But I'm attracted to you, more than to any woman I've ever met. I don't like the word *affair,* though. It sounds tacky, like 'What the hell, why not, we don't have anything better to do at the moment,' and what we would share wouldn't be like that. We can give and receive what we need, and there would be nothing, *nothing,* tacky about it."

Mark got to his feet and crossed the room to stand in front of Cedar.

"I didn't know I was lonely, either, until I met you. I want you, Cedar," he said, his voice husky. "I want to make love with you more than I can begin to tell you." He extended a hand toward her. "Please?"

This was good, and right and real, Cedar thought, as a wondrous warmth suffused her. They had been completely honest with each other so neither of them could be hurt or feel betrayed when what they were sharing was over. It would be theirs, as would the memories they could do with as they saw fit. Oh, she wanted this, wanted Mark, for as long as it lasted.

Cedar placed her hand in Mark's and rose to her feet.

"Yes," she said, smiling. "And to your please I add thank you."

Mark matched her smile for a moment, then dropped her hand to frame her face with both of his hands. His gaze swept over her face, slowly, slowly, as if he were etching each feature indelibly in his mind.

Finally, he lowered his head and kissed her, so tenderly, so reverently, that tears misted Cedar's eyes.

He broke the kiss to wrap his arms around her, nestling her to him as she raised her arms to encircle his shoulders. His mouth melted over hers once more in a kiss that was now searing with his want of her, his raging desire. Cedar answered the kiss in kind. They ended the kiss to draw much-needed breaths, then Cedar took Mark's hand and led him up the stairs to her bedroom.

It was as though they were encased in a magical, sensuous mist that kept the world beyond that room, beyond the two of them, at bay. This place was theirs and theirs alone.

Clothes became intolerable and were hastily removed and allowed to drop into puddles of material on the floor. Someone…her? him?…swept back the blankets on the bed and they tumbled onto cool, beckoning sheets, reaching immediately for each other.

They kissed, caressed, explored, and rejoiced in their discoveries. A body soft and feminine and one hard and tightly muscled seemed custom-made for each other.

Mark drew the lush bounty of one of Cedar's breasts into his mouth to lave the nipple to a tight bud that matched the tightening, coiling heat low in their bodies. He moved to the other breast, and Cedar relished the feel of the bunching muscles in his back beneath the palms of her fluttering hands.

He left her only long enough to protect her, then raised over her, then into her, filling her, bringing a sigh of pure pleasure from her lips.

The age-old dance of lovers began, the tempo slow, then gaining force to become a thundering rhythm that they matched beat for beat in exacting synchronization.

It was ecstasy.

It was like nothing they had known before.

It was theirs.

The heat and tension within them increased, bringing them closer to the climax they were reaching for. Closer now…closer…now soaring…clinging to each other…then flung away to oblivion seconds apart, each calling out the other's name.

They slowly drifted back to reality, too awed to speak, too sated to move. Mark gathered his last ounce of energy to shift to Cedar's side, tucking her close, then drawing the blankets over their cooling bodies. With heads resting on the same pillow, they slept.

But not for long.

"Cedar."

"Mmm."

"I have to go. I don't want to leave you, but I need to see the babysitter home and…tonight was incredible. I wish I was better with words so I could tell you how much…"

"I know. It was beautiful, Mark."

"Go back to sleep…and dream of me."

"I will, Mark. I will."

Chapter Seven

On Friday afternoon, when Bethany announced that Joey had arrived for his appointment, Cedar got to her feet, then sat right back down because of the trembling in her legs.

Get it together, she ordered herself. So what if she was about to see Mark for the first time since he'd left her bed.

She glanced at the roses, perched on top of the bookcase on the far wall, that Mark had sent to her office yesterday.

A dozen long-stem yellow roses in a lead crystal vase.

She smiled as she recalled, for the umpteenth time, the card that had accompanied the gorgeous bouquet.

"Thank you for a memorable evening. Mark."

Get it together, she ordered herself again, then strode across the room to open the door.

"Hello, Joey," she said from the doorway. "Mark."

"Hello, Cedar," Mark said, getting to his feet.

"'Lo," Joey mumbled, not moving.

"Mark, may I see you in my office for a moment, please?" Cedar said. "Joey, finish your yummy snack. I'll be right back."

Joey shrugged.

Mark entered the office and Cedar closed the door.

"I just wanted to thank you for the beautiful roses," she said quietly, glancing quickly at the door. "It was so lovely, so thoughtful of you to send them."

"I'm glad you like them," Mark said, smiling. "I know that red roses are more traditional, but the other night wasn't ordinary, not even close. When I went into the florist shop, I realized that red roses weren't going to cut it."

"You're…you're a romantic," Cedar said, smiling at him warmly.

"I am?" Mark said, frowning. "No, I'm not. I am? I never thought of myself as being a guy who did corny romantic stuff."

"There is nothing corny about those flowers, Mark."

"Oh." He grinned. "Well, I guess I can handle the label of romantic if it makes your eyes sparkle the way they are."

"Well…"

"Shh," he whispered as he wrapped his arms around her, pulling her close to his body, and kissed her deeply. Cedar wove her arms around Mark's waist and urged him even closer as she savored his taste, his feel, his aroma. When he finally broke the kiss, they both drew much-needed breaths.

"Gracious," Cedar said. "I…I've got to get going on Joey's session." She paused. "He didn't appear too happy to be here."

"He…" Mark said, then cleared his throat. "He was chattering about his buddy, Benny, when I picked him up, but the closer we got to your office, the more sullen he became. He likes you, Cedar, very much, but he's mentioned that you ask him too many questions."

Cedar sighed. "About things he doesn't want to face. I have to say, I'm not making the progress I'd hoped for. He still refuses to talk about his parents, about what happened."

"He won't at home, either. He's becoming more sociable, doesn't hide out in his room so much and we even made barbecue chicken together last night, but he hasn't said one word about my sister and brother-in-law."

Cedar nodded. "All right. Let's see what I can do during this session. Joey is my last client of the day. If things go better by any chance, will it inconvenience you if we run over our normal time?"

"Not at all. I'll just hit Bethany up for a snack."

"Okay," Cedar said, smiling.

"Cedar," Mark said, suddenly serious. "It's great to see you. I've thought about you a lot since the other night."

"I've…I've thought about you, too, Mark."

"Good. That's good."

"Joey," Cedar said, hearing the breathlessness in her voice. "Now."

"Right."

Fifteen minutes later, Cedar sat opposite Joey in one of the chairs that fronted her desk. She studied the little boy, who was examining a bandage on one of his fingers.

Not responding…again, Cedar thought. The walls were solidly in place…again. Oh, Joey.

"You know," Cedar said, "this isn't exactly fair,

is it? You come here and I ask you all sorts of questions. Let's change sides. You ask me something."

Joey switched his gaze from the bandage to Cedar.

"'Kay," he said. "Did Uncle Mark kiss you when you went to the fancy restaurant? I asked him and he said it was none of my business."

"Well, it's a rather private subject, that's all."

"How come grown-ups get private-subject stuff, but kids gotta answer questions about everything and nobody cares if it's private to them or not?"

"That's a very good point, Joey. You come to see me and I push you to talk to me, don't I?"

"Yeah."

"I think…yes, I think it's time you had someone else to speak to here instead of me."

"Who?" Joey said, sitting up straight in his chair, his eyes widening.

"A very special friend," Cedar said, rising to her feet.

She went to a closet and removed a four-foot clown painted on heavy-duty plastic that was weighted at the bottom. A happy smile was on its face and its clothes were brightly colored. Cedar set the object between her chair and Joey's.

"This," she said, "is Puncho. Watch this."

Cedar leaned forward to press the toy all the way to the floor. She released it and Puncho popped right back up to where he had been.

"Cool," Joey said, inching toward the edge of his chair.

"He always comes back up to see you," Cedar said, "and nothing, absolutely nothing makes him stop smiling. Yes, I agree, he is very cool. Aren't you, Puncho? Yep."

"Yeah," Joey said, his gaze riveted on the clown.

"Let me tell you a story, Joey," Cedar said. "When Oreo was a kitten, I received a beautiful sweater for my birthday. I had laid the sweater on my bed while I showered because I planned to wear it that day. When I got ready to putting it on, I discovered that Oreo had been playing on it and had snagged it with her claws. There were holes everywhere and my lovely gift was ruined."

"Wow," Joey said. "What did you do to Oreo?"

"Nothing, because it wasn't her fault. Kittens are kittens, and she couldn't be blamed for what happened. But, you know, I was so upset because I had lost something precious to me. I came to work and got Puncho out of the closet. I told him what Oreo had done, that I was sad about my sweater but that there was no one to be angry with. So…I hit him, really clobbered him, and he popped back up for more and kept on smiling because that's what he does. Oh, I felt so much better after that. You must understand, Joey, that we never hit people when we're upset. Never! I went home that night and hugged Oreo and everything was fine. Would you like to give Puncho a bit of a push?"

"No," Joey said, then shrugged. "Well, maybe just one."

"Go ahead."

Joey slid off the chair and stood in front of the clown. He placed his hand flat on Puncho's face and shoved the object back several inches. When he jerked his hand away, the clown returned to its original position.

"I know," Cedar said, laughing at the expression on Joey's face. "Tell Puncho about Uncle Mark's scrambled eggs."

Joey hesitated, then nodded.

"Uncle Mark…" he said, smacking the clown with a little more force—Puncho popped back up. "…makes." Punch. "The worst scrambled eggs." Punch. "In the whole wide world." Wham.

"Very good." Cedar clapped her hands.

"But Uncle Mark makes good barbecue chicken now," Joey said, looking at Cedar.

"You taught him well," she said. "What else do you want to tell Puncho? Mmm. Let's see. How about sharing with him the reason you're living in Phoenix with your Uncle Mark?"

"Puncho doesn't care about that."

"Sweetie, Puncho cares about everything. He let me go on and on about my sweater, remember? Go ahead, Joey, tell him why you're living here."

Please, Joey, Cedar silently begged, give way to your pain. Cry, my darling little boy. Cry and cry and cry.

"Well...yeah...okay. Uncle Mark brought me here," Joey said, giving the clown a light shove, "because I didn't have anywhere else to go." He hit Puncho with more force. "I didn't because...because..." He slammed Puncho in the nose. "...my mom...mom...and...dad..." He curled his hands into fists and hit Puncho with the left, then the right. "...*died*. They went in the car and got themself killed and..." He landed another punch, then another. "...and left me all alone."

Cedar pressed the fingertips of one hand to her lips.

"They shouldn't have done that," Joey yelled, again slamming one fist then the other into Puncho, who popped back up for more. "No. No. No. I hate them for doing that. *I hate them.*" Sweat trickled down Joey's face as he hit the clown over and over and over. "If they really loved me, they wouldn't have gone away forever, and left me forever to be scared and stuff."

Joey kicked the clown, then hit him again and

again. "Why did they do that?" he screamed. "Why…did…they…do that?"

Then Joey looked at Cedar and burst into tears. "Cedar?" he said, sobbing, "how come they did that?"

"Oh, thank God," she said, her own eyes filling with tears. She opened her arms to Joey. "Come here, baby."

Joey rushed into Cedar's embrace and she lifted him onto her lap, holding him tightly as he cried as if his heart was breaking into a million pieces. He clung to her, great racking sobs sweeping through his tiny body.

"They didn't want to leave you, Joey," she said close to his ear. "They loved you so much, they truly did. The accident wasn't their fault. *They are not to blame for leaving you.* It wasn't Oreo's fault she ruined my sweater and made me sad. It wasn't your mom and dad's fault they left you and made you so very, very sad.

"But, sweetheart, they made certain that if anything *did* happen to them, you would live with someone who loved you just as they did. Your Uncle Mark. He does love you, Joey. He does. He makes mistakes sometimes because he doesn't have any practice at being a daddy, but he's trying so hard, he really is. He wants you to be happy, to smile again, to laugh and play."

Two tears spilled onto Cedar's cheeks.

"Now you have a new forever, honey," she continued. "You're Uncle Mark's little boy. That doesn't mean you should forget your mom and dad and how much you loved them and they loved you. But it does mean that you're not alone, you're with someone who loves you with all his heart. Uncle Mark makes crummy scrambled eggs, but he's learning how to cook and he's learning how to be a dad…a forever dad, Joey. For you."

Cedar placed her cheek on Joey's head, inhaling his all-boy aroma of healthy, sweaty hair and soap. She tightened her hold on him even more, knowing, rejoicing in the fact that he was now on the road to healing.

Because Joey had cried.

"Joey, do you believe that your Uncle Mark loves you?"

Joey drew a shuddering, sobbing breath.

"Yeah," he whispered. "Yeah, he does, Cedar. He does. Even…even when…he's grumpy."

Joey's eyes drifted closed and his hands loosened their hold on her as he fell into a deep, exhausted sleep, his tearstained face nestled against her breast. Cedar looked at a grinning Puncho.

"Thank you, my friend," she said softly.

She sat in the chair for another ten minutes, holding Joey while he slept. Then she slipped an arm under his knees, lifting him as she stood, and managed to press the button on the intercom at the edge of the desk.

"Mark," she said.

Seconds later, the office door opened and Mark strode into the room with a panicked expression on his face.

"What…" he started.

"Shh," Cedar said, moving forward.

They met in the middle of the room. Mark looked at Joey, then the clown, before switching his gaze to Cedar, an expression of confusion and concern on his face.

"What happened?" he said, his voice hushed. "What's wrong? What's going on here?"

Cedar managed to produce a wobbly smile as fresh tears filled her eyes.

"Joey cried," she said. "Oh, Mark, it's a major emotional breakthrough for him. We'll have to be very careful as we proceed since he could put those walls right back up. But he poured out his heart and revealed his anger and pain to Puncho the clown. It's good." She nodded. "It's very, very good."

Mark stared at Joey again.

"He's wiped out," he said. "Ah, man, he looks so small, so helpless. There're tears on his face and…" He met Cedar's gaze again, his frown deepening. He reached up and drew a thumb over one of her cheeks, wiping away the tears. "You're crying, too. This is ripping me up."

"It's all right, Mark," Cedar said. "I can usually remain objective with my clients, but Joey…Joey is so special. He…oh, I don't know…he latched on to my heart the first time we met and…" She smiled. "…I don't think he's going to let go."

"You're an incredible lady," Mark said, his voice gritty as a foreign tightness seized his throat.

And you latched on to my heart the first time we met, Cedar Kennedy, he thought, with an edge of franticness. I think I might…maybe…oh, cripe, I think I'm falling in love with you. Damn it, give me my heart back because…oh, hell.

"Mark?" Cedar said questioningly. "What is it? You look so stricken all of a sudden and the color just drained from your face and…what's wrong?"

"What's wrong?" Mark repeated, running his hand over the back of his neck. "Um…well, you said Joey could put his walls back in place and I'm afraid I'll mess up, you know? Say or do something that will blow the progress you made today and…I'm really out of my element here."

In more ways than one, he thought.

"We'll take it slow and easy," Cedar said. "You're not alone in this, Mark. I'm here. For Joey. For…

you." She paused. "Would you take Joey, please? He's getting rather heavy."

"Geez, I'm sorry," Mark said. "I'm standing here like a dolt while you…let me have him."

Cedar leaned forward with her precious bundle as Mark slid one arm across Joey's back and another under his knees, his arms pressing against hers. Their faces were only inches apart as they supported the sleeping little boy together. Their eyes met, held, and time stopped.

Dear heaven, Cedar thought, as swirling heat consumed her, she had to move, put some distance between her and Mark before she went up in flames. He'd kissed her earlier, here, in her office, and she shouldn't have allowed that to happen. She had to keep the professional separate from the personal. She had to. Somehow.

She tore her gaze from Mark's and slid her arms free, watching as he cradled Joey against his chest. She took a step backward and wrapped her hands around her elbows.

"You'll have to play the evening by ear," she said stiffly, looking at a spot over Mark's shoulder. "Don't broach the subject of what happened here today. Wait and see if Joey brings it up. If he doesn't, leave it alone for now. If he chatters like a magpie, listen to him. If he—"

"I get the picture," Mark said, frowning. "Why are you getting into your shrinky-dink mode all of a sudden?"

Cedar planted her hands on her hips. "I beg your pardon?"

Joey stirred in Mark's arms, then settled again.

"I am *not*," Cedar said, keeping her voice down, "in my shrinky-dink mode as you so indelicately put it. I'm simply giving you instructions as to how to proceed with Joey this evening. He's so exhausted by what took place here, he could very well sleep through until morning and that's fine. Any questions?"

"Yeah," Mark said, "I do have a question. What are you afraid of, Cedar? Talk about walls. Man, if I could build them that fast with my crew, I'd be a millionaire. I saw the desire in your eyes when we were both holding Joey. I felt the heat, the…then you backed off, got all stiff and snooty, whipping your professional stuff at me."

"I…"

"Joey and I are a package deal, Cedar. Did *I* stake a claim on part of your heart, too? Is that what's got you scrambling for safety behind the wall you just slammed into place between us?"

"No, of course not," she said, lifting her chin and taking another step backward. "We both understand that what's happening between us is temporary. I am *not* afraid of anything, Mr. Chandler."

Except the fact that you consume my thoughts when we're apart, she thought miserably, and light up my life when I see you again. You're tiptoeing around my heart, Mark but you can't have it. No. Not now. Not ever.

"Look," she said wearily, "I'm just as exhausted as Joey is at the moment. Take Joey home. I'll see you both on Monday for his regular session."

"What about you and me, together, at some point during the weekend?"

"That wouldn't be a good idea," she said. "Joey needs your undivided attention right now. He might be frightened by the emotions that surfaced here today. Just concentrate on your...son. That's who he is, you know, because you've taken over the role of being his father."

"Yeah, well, the last I heard fathers are men," Mark said, "and this man wants to see you."

Cedar laughed in spite of her frazzled state.

"You're pouting," she said. "Shame on you."

Mark matched her smile. "So, send me to my room. That's fine as long as you come with me."

"Shoo," Cedar said, flapping her hands at him. "Take that beautiful boy home and spend the weekend showering him with TLC."

"I guess that means I can't slip any scrambled eggs into the menu."

"Don't even think about it."

"Okay. I'm outta here." Mark paused. "Thank you, Cedar, for what you did for Joey today, and for me as his… father. Father. Great dad I am. I don't have a clue what I'm doing."

"Just love him, Mark."

"Love solves everything, huh?"

"Most of the time it does…at least for little boys and girls, with a bit of help here and there from shrinky-dinks like me. It's the grown-ups that complicate things." Cedar waved a hand in the air. "See, I told you I was tired. I'm babbling. Goodbye until Monday."

Mark stared at her for a long, thoughtful moment, then nodded. "Until Monday," he said, turning toward the door.

Cedar moved around him to open the door, then watched him leave with Joey cradled safely in his arms.

She would not, must not, fall in love with that man. She had to stay alert, because she was a breath away from losing her heart to Mark Chandler and she wasn't going to allow that to happen. No. Absolutely not.

Cedar glanced at her watch and saw that it was

well past office hours. She collected her purse from the bottom drawer of her desk, turned off the lights in her office and started across the now-empty reception area for the main door to the suite. As she reached for the handle, the door opened. Gasping, she jerked back in surprise.

"Oh, Cedar, I'm sorry," her late-night visitor said. "I just took a chance that I might catch you before you left. I didn't mean to scare you to death."

"You definitely got my attention, Kathy," Cedar said, smiling at the attractive young woman. "What's so urgent on a Friday night?"

"Could we sit down for a second?" Kathy said. "It's been a long day and my feet are killing me. I really need to speak to you, though. Were you rushing home to get ready for a date tonight?"

"No," Cedar said quietly. "I don't have any plans. Sit down and talk to me."

Kathy settled onto the sofa in the reception area and Cedar sat in a chair opposite her so they could easily communicate.

"You know I'm Cindy Swanson's social worker," Kathy said, "or case manager, to use the official jargon."

Cedar nodded.

"Well, I made a routine visit to her foster home this afternoon. As you're aware, I managed to place

Cindy with Pearl Carson, a gem of a foster mom. I could use about a hundred more like Pearl. Anyway, I spoke with Cindy privately, then Pearl alone, then the two of them together, which is how I like to do home visits."

"And?" Cedar said. "Are you here because there's a problem with my approach to Cindy and her situation?"

"No, no, nothing like that," Kathy said. "You're doing a terrific job with Cindy. That homework assignment you gave her about the cost of apartments and day care was brilliant. It was definitely reality-check time for that young lady."

"It's worked well for me with other young pregnant girls," Cedar said. "They have no idea what they are really facing and—never mind. Let's zero in on why you're here. As you said, it's been a long day."

"Aren't they all?" Kathy said, sighing. "Okay, Cedar, here it is in a nutshell. Cindy is very adamant about you adopting her baby. She said that you're thinking it over and she has decided that if you won't adopt her baby girl, then she's going to keep it because she refuses to allow anyone else to have that child."

Cedar opened her mouth, then closed it again as she realized she was at a complete loss for words.

"When I spoke with Pearl privately," Kathy continued, "she told me that Cindy is solid on this point. Pearl is a twenty-year veteran of these wars and I have complete confidence in her ability to read her foster kids."

"Oh, but…" Cedar started, then just stopped speaking and stared at Kathy.

"The thing is, Cedar," Kathy said, "the birth mother has the final say in who gets her baby should she go the adoption route. You know that. She can interview a zillion couples, or single moms or dads, or whoever from the applications, and then she makes her choice."

"I know, but…"

"That cookie is not kidding," Kathy said. "Cindy will keep that baby, heaven help it, if you don't adopt her. I don't think you and I have ever discussed the topic of having kids someday, but you wouldn't have chosen your specialty in your field if you didn't like the little darlings.

"Anyway, Cindy said you agreed to think about adoption and I need to know where your head is. You'd pass CPS and state requirements to adopt with flying colors.

"Oh, before I forget," Kathy continued. "The one stipulation that Cindy has is that you have bunny wallpaper in the baby's nursery. You gotta love these fifteen-year-old mothers-to-be. They are operating on another planet at times. Anyway, there's paperwork to set in motion if you're a go on this, and a home study to do. You know the drill.

"Actually, this is rather exciting. You and I have been friends for years. I'll get to be an auntie who spoils your kid rotten, while you do all the diaper detail. Works for me. So, Cedar? Speak to me."

"I…I don't know what to say," Cedar said. "I *sort* of told Cindy I'd think about adopting her baby, but…no, I didn't actually say that, but…" She pressed one hand to her forehead for a moment. "This is overwhelming. Cindy has definitely made up her mind that…oh, my. A baby girl. A baby. That was a forgotten dream, a broken dream, a…oh, but, Kathy, I work such long hours and…well, I *could* cut back a bit and…but my house is falling apart. Then again, I *was* planning on selling it and getting something newer, with a backyard for a little girl to play in and…no, this is ridiculous. I'm in no position to…a baby. A precious baby girl that could actually be mine? A baby to hold tightly in my arms just the way I did with Joey?"

"Who?" Kathy said.

"Never mind. I'm slipping over the edge. I have to think this through." Cedar paused. "What about the legalities of my being Cindy's therapist? I might have brainwashed her."

"No problem," Kathy said, rising from the sofa. "There are enough of us who know you and Cindy to nip that idea in the bud. So, okay, take the whole weekend to think."

"That's all the time I get?" Cedar said, jumping to her feet. "What's the rush?"

"The fact that if Cindy is willing to put her baby up for adoption, her mother is ready to have her come home now instead of after the baby is born," Kathy said. "That would get Cindy out of the foster-care system and back where she belongs. Pearl is wonderful, but I'm sure you'd agree that Cindy would be better off with her own mother, who is really a super lady. She just had enough to deal with without Cindy insisting on keeping the baby. Cindy wants to have this child, know it's with you, safe and loved, and go back to being fifteen years old. When is Cindy's next session with you?"

"Monday afternoon."

"Perfect. I'll call you here Monday morning and find out what you've decided to do." Kathy gave Cedar a quick hug. "Say yes. You'd be a terrific mother, Cedar. That would be one lucky baby, no doubt about it. Have a…thoughtful weekend. 'Bye for now."

Kathy left the office and Cedar sank back into the chair. Her trembling legs had refused to hold her for another second. She wrapped her hands around her elbows and remembered what it had felt like to hold Joey in her arms, the yearning that had consumed her, the irrational wish that he was hers, that she didn't have to give him back to Mark.

Mark. Magnificent Mark. He was trying so hard to be a good father to Joey. Mark, who had put aside his manly pride to ask for help so Joey could be a happy little boy again. Mark, who would be a wonderful father for Joey, and for the children he would create with the woman he chose to be his wife.

Mark, who would never be a part of her forever because—

Cedar drew a shuddering breath.

Marrying again, being an equal partner with a special man, was not going to happen. Ever. It was a shattered dream, just as being a mother was.

But now, a precious baby girl could be hers. A daughter. Half of her broken dream was hers for the having if she agreed to adopt Cindy's child.

Dear heaven, was it fair to take that baby knowing she would never have a father? But the alternative was a mother who really didn't want that role, who wanted to have a pretty dress and go to the school dance.

Cedar pressed her fingertips to her aching temples.

She was exhausted, she knew. She was just chasing her own thoughts around in circles in her mind. A good night's sleep would make things clearer and enable her, she hoped, to make the right decision.

She wished she could talk it all through with someone. Pour out her heart to a person who cared about her. Her mother would listen, but her mom was so eager to be a grandmother, there was no way she would be objective. She'd want to get off the telephone as quickly as possible so she could rush to the store for yarn to start knitting booties for her granddaughter.

And her girlfriends? They'd no doubt react as Kathy had. They'd view the whole thing as a fun adventure, encouraging her to go for it so they could be aunties with license to spoil the new arrival.

Well, she thought dryly, as she got to her feet, turned off the lights and locked the door behind her, she could always go home and pro and con the dilemma with Oreo. As long as she fed the cat first, Oreo was a very good listener.

Oh, who was she kidding? She knew who she wanted to talk this all through with. Mark Chandler. But she had told him to focus entirely on Joey this weekend, which was exactly what he should do.

No, the decision about the baby was hers alone to make.

Chapter Eight

The next afternoon, Cedar sat at her kitchen table scrutinizing the papers spread out before her. She'd spent the morning roaming through model homes at a new subdivision a few miles from where she now lived. She'd collected a handful of floor plans, price sheets, advertisements from institutions offering varying mortgage rates, as well as flyers from interior decorators, landscapers, and on and on from the pile of material in the model being used as an office—an office that featured a large sign stating that the homes were being built by Chandler Construction.

The woman in the office had made clear that the floor plans of the existing models were simply suggestions. Buyers could dictate the size of the rooms, their location within the house, and make any other changes to suit their needs.

Cedar pulled one of the floor plans forward, realizing that it was the third time she had reached for that particular design.

"Master bedroom," she said, tapping the labeled area on the paper with one fingertip, then moving her finger to another area on the sheet. "This room would be an office and guest-room combination and..." She shifted the paper closer and smiled. "...here is the baby's nursery, complete with bunny wallpaper."

Cedar plunked one elbow on the table, rested her chin in her hand and stared into space.

How strange was the human mind, she mused, or perhaps, in this case, the human heart. She'd gone to bed last night a befuddled, gloomy mess, so tired her bones ached. But when Oreo had nudged her awake early this morning announcing it was time for breakfast, everything changed.

She'd registered an immediate sense of rightness and inner peace about adopting Cindy's baby girl. While sleeping, her subconscious had taken over... perhaps with the help of whispering angels?...and the answer was waiting for her upon awakening. She was going to be a mother. It was meant to be.

No, she would never be a wife, but regaining half of her shattered dream was wonderful, and she was very grateful and excited about the impending birth of a daughter.

Oh, she wasn't kidding herself, she thought. Being a single parent was not going to be easy, but she'd deal with problems as they came and find solutions, just as the multitude of single moms did everyday.

A baby, she thought, sighing wistfully. A precious miracle to hold in her arms, just as she'd held special little Joey. Oh, how she adored that boy.

Thanks to Puncho, the clown, Joey had turned an emotional corner and was now on the right path toward healing the pain of losing his parents. There were still rough times ahead, but she'd be there to help Mark and Joey smooth troubled waters.

Cedar swept her gaze over the papers before her. Of its own volition, it seemed, her hand floated outward and slid another floor plan over the one she had been scrutinizing. This design was of a much larger house, with more and bigger rooms.

"Master bedroom," Cedar said, tapping the paper. "And this is the nursery, here is Joey's room, and over here is another room with enough space for a guest bed, plus two computer tables, mine and Mark's. Living room, family room and—oh!"

Oreo jumped onto the table and sat down on the piece of paper. The cat stared at Cedar, then me-owed.

"Okay, okay," Cedar said, "I get the message. I'm being silly and fanciful and you don't approve. Well, I have news for you, fat cat. I don't approve of you being on the table, so move your tush. Oreo, go."

The cat jumped back to the floor and strutted away, tail held high. Cedar looked at the floor plan again and shook her head in self-disgust.

Why had she sat there playing let's-pretend about something that would never ever happen, she wondered. She should be counting her blessings about becoming a mother, not daydreaming about having more, greedy woman that she was. Surely her sub-conscious hadn't planted that seed of hope during the night. No, that was ridiculous.

The telephone rang and Cedar got quickly to her feet, glad to be pulled from her nonsensical thoughts. She snatched up the receiver on the kitchen wall.

"Hello?"

"Cedar? This is Mark."

"Oh." She snapped her head around to look at the floor plan for the larger house, a warm flush staining her cheeks. "I…hello, Mark. Is something wrong?"

"I have a problem and I really need your help."

"Is it Joey?" she said, her hold on the receiver tightening.

"Yes. No. I mean, he's fine at the moment, playing with his Game Boy in the living room, not holed up in his bedroom."

"That's good," Cedar said. "So what's the problem?"

"Moose just called. He went to one of our sites to receive a shipment of bathroom fixtures from a guy who rolled in from Tucson. The thing is, they are the wrong ones. The guy said he'd take them back down there, but couldn't make the return trip until late Monday because they limit his overtime. We need those fixtures on the job first thing Monday morning to stay on schedule."

"And?" Cedar said, narrowing her eyes.

"Moose can't go to Tucson because it's his kid's birthday today and he promised to be at her party. So, well, I'm going to make the drive. My sitter is busy, so I was wondering if, maybe, you could take care of Joey? I thought about hauling him along with me, but it's a pretty boring stretch of highway and how many hours can a kid play with a Game Boy?"

"Mark, I thought you understood that all of your

attention should be centered on Joey this weekend because of what happened with him in my office yesterday. It's important that you stay close to him in case he wants to talk."

"I know that, but he hasn't said one word about his parents and you said not to push him. I'll only be gone for the day and this is an emergency. Give me a break here, Cedar. I had Chandler Construction before Joey came into my life. I can't put my business on the back burner at the drop of a hat. I have a reputation to protect, future job opportunities that depend on my maintaining a level of excellence. I'm talking about financial security for me and for Joey in the years ahead."

"Can't someone else make the drive to Tucson?" Cedar said. "You're a father now, Mark, just like Moose is. Joey shouldn't be put on the back burner, either."

"I'm doing this for Joey," Mark said, an edge to his voice. "Every dollar I put in the bank is security for what he will need down the road. There won't be any dollars if I start blowing my reputation of bringing jobs in on time. I'm the boss. I own the company. It's up to me to step up when there's a problem like this one."

Cedar sighed. "I think you need to examine your priorities a bit, Mark, but this isn't the time. Yes, all right. Bring Joey over and I'll take care of him. I hope this doesn't upset him."

"Hey, he's crazy about you, Cedar. He won't care if I leave."

Joey definitely cared.

When Cedar opened her front door, Joey stomped past her, his arms crossed over his chest and a stormy expression on his face. He marched into the living room and slouched onto the sofa.

"Hi," Mark said, producing a small smile as he entered the house.

"Mmm," Cedar said, glaring at him.

"Emergencies happen, Cedar," Mark said, keeping his voice low. "Don't look at me like I'm an axe murderer or something. Joey's old enough to understand that things don't always go as planned."

"He's very fragile right now, Mark," Cedar whispered. "He needs stability in his life and promises that get kept. What did you tell him you two were going to do together this afternoon?"

Mark hooked a hand on the back of his neck. "Buy a kite and fly it over at the park near our house," he said. "He flew kites with Moose's kids when we were there for Thanksgiving and really liked it. Hey, I told him we can do that tomorrow."

"You don't get it," Cedar said. "You just don't get

it. Later, when Joey is more steady on his emotional feet, things can be postponed or changed because of circumstances beyond your control, but not now."

"I have a business to run," Mark said, his voice rising.

"Shh."

"Well, cripe, I happen to think that financial security is just as important as...as emotional security, or whatever shrinky-dink term you want to use. Chandler Construction is going to make it possible for Joey to have everything he needs, including a college education. The money his parents' estate left for him won't last forever. I'm making certain he won't do without one thing."

"Except your time and attention."

"This is an emergency!"

"Fine," Cedar said, throwing up her hands. "I give up. I can't get through to you. Go get your cute little faucets or whatever it is that is so vitally important."

"I intend to," Mark said, frowning. "May I have a drink of water before I hit the road?"

Cedar swept an arm toward the kitchen, indicating very clearly that Mark should get his own glass of water. He strode toward the kitchen, glancing quickly at Joey who hadn't moved since flopping onto the sofa. Cedar looked at sullen Joey, as well, then followed Mark into the kitchen, where she found Mark staring at the papers on the table.

"What's all this?" he said, nodding toward the materials.

"I told you I wanted to get a newer house because this one is driving me crazy," she said. "This morning, out of curiosity, I explored that subdivision going up near here. It would be quite a challenge to have a home built from scratch with all those decisions to make."

Mark smiled. "Well, you wouldn't have to worry about the quality of your home. I happen to know that Chandler Construction is the best of the bunch."

"Do tell," she said, laughing in spite of herself. "Don't break your arm patting yourself on the back."

Mark's smile disappeared.

"I've earned my top-of-the-line reputation by dedication and hard work, Cedar," he said. "At some point, I'll be able to ease up on my responsibilities, delegate more, but not yet. Not until I reach my goal of financial security.

"In fact, I need to reevaluate that goal because of Joey. That ease-up phase of my life may be pushed back."

"But Joey needs you *now*, Mark."

"I take off early to get him to the appointments with you. Don't I get any credit for that?"

"Yes, of course, but…never mind. We'll talk about

this another time. You need to get going to Tucson. Did you have your water?"

"Water?" he said absently as he picked up a sheet from the table. "Yes. I had plenty." He paused. "This is the floor plan for a pretty big house. Is this the one you're considering buying?"

"I...um...no. I don't need something that large. I'm not even certain I want to take on all the details of a brand-new place like that. It boggles my mind."

"I'd help you if you really wanted to have a home customized to your heart's desire. I'd walk you through the whole process. You deserve to have what you want, Cedar."

What I want, she thought, feeling the unwelcome prickle of tears, is that house on the paper in your hand. I want to fill it with love and laughter and a family made up of you, me, Joey and the baby that's on the way. What I want, Mark, is not to have fallen in love with you, but I did, I know that now, and I'm so mad at myself, I could just scream. So, go get your dumb faucets and leave me alone.

"Cedar?" Mark said, dropping the paper back onto the table to stare at her. "Where did you go?"

"What? Oh, sorry. I was just thinking about houses and...stuff. I need to get this monster on the market, too." She paused. "Well, try to make peace with Joey before you leave."

"Yes, ma'am." Mark walked to where she stood, dropped a quick kiss on her lips, then headed into the living room.

Cedar pressed the fingertips of one hand to lips that still tingled from the kiss. Then she went to the table, turned the floor plan for the large house over with a smack and went into the living room.

"He's not speaking to me," Mark said. "Nothing. Nada. Nope."

"Joey," Cedar said, "I know you're disappointed about not flying the kite today and…" She glared at Mark. "…for good reason. However, that doesn't give you a free ticket to be rude. Say goodbye to your Uncle Mark."

"'Bye," Joey said, staring straight ahead.

Mark threw up his hands and headed toward the front door.

"Whoever said women are difficult hasn't dealt with a ticked-off seven-year-old boy," he yelled. "I'm outta here, people. I'll be back as soon as I can. I love you. Adios. Goodbye."

I love you, too, Mark, Cedar thought, then cringed as the front door slammed. Because Mark's declaration of love had been directed toward Joey, not her, and she knew it. There she went, playing mind games again. Ridiculous.

"Well, Mr. Crabby Apple," she said cheerfully,

"have you had your afternoon snack yet? I happen to have Rocky Road ice cream in the freezer."

Joey's head snapped up. "Really? Rocky Road?" He slid off the sofa. "Cool."

"Joey," Cedar said, when he reached her side, "your Uncle Mark wouldn't be going to Tucson if it wasn't an emergency."

"People shouldn't break promises, Cedar. They shouldn't. He promised me that we'd get the kite and fly it. Today. Not tomorrow. Today. Promises are important. They're like forever stuff, you know?"

"I know, sweetheart," she said gently. "Well, come on. Let's dig into that ice cream."

Mark managed to concentrate on maneuvering the truck through the city traffic. But when he took the off ramp and joined the parade of vehicles moving at a steady pace along I-10 toward Tucson, the words he had spoken as he left Cedar's house once again occupied his mind.

I'll be back as soon as I can. I love you. Adios. Goodbye… I love you. I love you. I love…

"Damn," he said, smacking the steering wheel with the palm of his hand.

Cedar would assume that his declaration of love had been directed only at Joey. But that wasn't the case. Nope. The truth had come right out of his mouth.

He was in love with Cedar Kennedy.

A knot had tightened in his gut when he saw the floor plans on Cedar's table. He didn't want Cedar to buy a new house, move into it with just her cat Oreo. He wanted her to pack up and settle into the home he was sharing with Joey.

That was what it would be if Cedar was there, a home. They'd be a real family. Mom, Dad, son and more babies to come in the future. They'd be Mr. and Mrs. Mark Chandler. Cedar Kennedy Chandler. It had a nice ring to it.

He sure was painting a pretty picture in his mind of all of them together, Mark mused, but it wasn't going to happen. In the first place, he had no idea how deeply Cedar's feelings for him ran. It really helped if the bride was in love with the groom, which might not be remotely close to how she felt. Plus, they'd agree that a serious relationship was not in the cards for them, that any feelings, emotions, whatever would *not* be mentioned.

Second, it was the wrong time in his life for where his wayward thoughts were taking him. He hadn't yet reached his financial goals.

Third, he was already wiggling things around to make space for Joey in his life, to learn how to be a father to a troubled and sad little boy. Love between a man and a woman had to be nurtured, like a...

flower garden. Geez, how corny, he thought, but true. The way things stood now, he was just barely keeping up with his paperwork by working in his home office after Joey went to bed. He'd fallen behind by taking off early to get Joey to his appointments with Cedar, and he couldn't allow that to happen.

A husband and a father spent his evenings with his family. He got home in time to have dinner with them, no matter what. He devoted the remaining hours of his day to his kids, and his wife. He didn't work weekends, that was for sure.

He knew all that, knew how it should be. The problem was, there weren't enough hours in the day for him to fit in everything and everyone. Chandler Construction was still growing, and he was grateful for that. Each bid he won, each new project he started, represented money in the bank, security for himself and now for Joey.

But, damn it, he was in love for the first time in his life with a woman who was more fantastic than anyone he had ever hoped to find. What about that?

Mark's shoulders slumped and a headache began to pound.

What about that? his mind echoed. It didn't matter. He'd found the perfect woman at the wrong time in his life. He wasn't ready, hadn't reached his goals, couldn't even dream about a future with Cedar because there wasn't going to be one.

He'd have to settle for whatever they shared before they decided to call it quits and went their separate ways. He'd have to settle for memories and the taunting thoughts of what might have been.

I'll be back as soon as I can. I love you. Good-bye.

Mark sighed and pressed harder on the gas pedal. He would get back from Tucson as soon as he could. But he wouldn't be saying 'I love you' to Cedar.

And somewhere down the road he and Cedar would say goodbye.

Joey's chipper mood at the prospect of having Rocky Road ice cream had lasted only as long as the treat. Once the bowls were rinsed and in the dishwasher, he once again slouched onto the sofa with a frown. Nothing Cedar suggested they do together tempted him. He was hurt and angry because his Uncle Mark had broken a promise and that was that.

"Joey," Cedar said finally, "I have a suggestion. Want to hear it?"

Joey shrugged.

"I was thinking that you should have your very own Puncho the clown to keep in your bedroom at your house. Then if you were upset the way you are now, you could tell Puncho and feel better again. Yes?"

"Well, maybe," Joey said, then looked at Cedar. "Okay. Yeah. Cool."

"Great. We'll buy another Puncho, then stop by my office because I have an air pump to blow him up."

"It will be *my* Puncho?" Joey said, sliding off the sofa. "To keep forever?"

"Yep."

"I can hit him or hug him, or do whatever I want to because he's all mine?"

"Right."

"Forever? Promise?"

"Forever, Joey," Cedar said, her heart aching for this fragile little boy who meant so very, very much to her. "I promise."

By the time their mission was accomplished, it was time for dinner. Cedar made spaghetti and garlic toast, and, with his very own Puncho smiling in the chair next to him at the table, Joey ate a big serving of each.

"You make great spaghetti, Cedar," Joey said, when his plate was clean.

"Well, thank you, sir," she said, smiling. "I'm glad you enjoyed it."

"I wish you lived with me and Uncle Mark, Cedar."

"Because I cook better than your Uncle Mark?" Cedar said, laughing.

"Well, yeah, but that's not all," Joey said. "Uncle Mark smiles more when he's around you. He's happier, or something, and not so grumpy. I think he likes you a lot, and I like you a lot, and you like us 'cause I can tell you do, so it's a good idea that you live with us, see?"

Sold, Cedar thought. Oh, if only seven-year-old boys could rule the world.

"Joey," Cedar said, reaching across the table to cover one of his hands with one of hers, "listen to me carefully. Okay?"

"'Kay."

"Your mom and dad lived together because they were in love with each other, got married, then later had you. That's how it works. Now, not all families are the same. Some kids have a mom and dad, some have just a dad, some have just a mom, some even live with their grandparents."

Joey nodded.

"You had a mom and dad, Joey, and it's understandable that you're sad because things changed so much. But you're not alone. You have your Uncle Mark, who is learning to be your new dad."

"And you could be my new mom, Cedar," Joey said, pulling his hand free of hers. "You could if you wanted to. Why don't you want to?"

"I explained it already, Joey. Your Uncle Mark and I are not…we're not in love with each other, we're not going to get married. You and Uncle Mark are a terrific family together, and it will just get better and better."

"Couldn't you try and fall in love with Uncle Mark?" Joey said, leaning toward her. "And I could ask him to try and fall in love with you."

"No," Cedar said, getting to her feet and picking up the plates. "That's not how it works. You'll have to trust me on this one, kiddo. You just concentrate on making things good in your family with Uncle Mark. Okay? Okay. End of discussion, sir. We polished off the ice cream already. Why don't you get that package of cookies out of the cupboard for our dessert?"

"But…"

"Cookies, Joey. Now."

"Yeah," Joey said, with a dejected sigh, "okay."

Thank goodness, Cedar thought, plunking the plates on the counter. One more minute of Joey's dissertation and she would have burst into tears, wailing to the rooftops that she was already in love with his Uncle Mark but that he didn't love her and never would if he knew…no, she wasn't going to go there…because the family Joey was desperately trying to construct just wasn't going to happen. Ever.

Think about the baby girl you're going to have, she ordered herself, and count your blessings. Joey's dream was a pipe dream.

Chapter Nine

At eight o'clock that night, Joey was still at Cedar's house, standing by the front window and peering out at the darkness beyond. He had one arm wrapped around Puncho the clown, the toy never far from his side.

"Joey," Cedar said, coming up behind him, "you've been standing there for nearly a half hour. I know you're concerned because Uncle Mark isn't back yet, but when you think about it, he didn't say what time he thought he would get here. There's no reason to be worried."

"It's dark already," Joey said. "Uncle Mark said he'd be back as soon as he could. This isn't soon, Cedar. It isn't. Bad stuff can happen when people drive in the dark. Sometimes...sometimes they don't ever come back because...because they got in an accident and then they're dead and are gone forever and...I want my Uncle Mark." He burst into tears.

Cedar dropped to her knees and turned Joey toward her. He flung his arms around her neck, buried his face in her shoulder and wept.

Mark Chandler, if you're at some truck stop on the highway having dinner and shooting the breeze with the good ol' boys, I'm going to strangle you with my bare hands, Cedar thought.

"Joey, honey, listen to me," she said, rubbing his back. "You're tired because it's your bedtime. How about a bubble bath for you and Puncho? Then you can sleep in my guest room. Cool, huh?"

"No," Joey mumbled, then sniffled. "I'm going to wait right here by the window for Uncle Mark."

Cedar sighed. She pulled Joey's arms gently from her neck and moved him back slightly to look at his tear-streaked face. "All right," she said. "I'll stay here with you and Puncho. We'll watch for Uncle Mark together."

"'Kay."

Cedar moved two chairs by the window, then

opened the curtains that Joey had been pushing aside.

"Oh, look at the stars," she said. "They're like diamonds sparkling in the sky. I don't see the moon, though. Do you?"

"No," Joey said, not shifting his gaze heavenward.

"Maybe it's behind a cloud. Hey, Mr. Moon, come out, come out wherever you are. We want to say hello. Joey, why don't you call to the moon?"

"No."

So much for that, Cedar thought. Oh, yes, Mr. Chandler, when I get you alone, you are going to get a piece of my mind, buster.

"Cedar, look, look," Joey said, pointing out the window. "In the driveway. See? Lights. It's Uncle Mark. It is, Cedar."

Before Cedar could stop him, Joey ran across the room and out the front door. She nearly fell over Puncho in her attempt to follow Joey, then regained her footing and hurried after him.

From the light spilling out the front door she could see Joey fling himself at Mark, who picked him up and carried him toward the house. Joey's legs were wrapped around Mark's chest and his arms encircled his uncle's neck in a tight hold.

"I'm here, buddy," Mark said to Joey. "Everything is fine."

As Mark entered the house with his armload of little boy, Cedar glared at him, then shut the door.

"I can explain," Mark said to Cedar.

"I'm not the one who is falling apart because you're so late," she said stiffly. "I realize you didn't tell us an approximate time for your return, but it's after eight o'clock, Mark. In case you're missing the message, that is a very upset child you're holding there." She sat down in an easy chair and crossed her arms beneath her breasts.

Mark walked to the sofa and sat down, as well. He shifted Joey sideways on his lap, frowning when he saw the tear tracks on Joey's face.

"Joey," Mark said, "listen to me. Okay, buddy? Will you do that much? Hear what I have to say?"

Joey shrugged and stared at Mark's shirt.

"Right," Mark said wearily. "Well, this is the scoop. I got to the supplier's place in Tucson and... guess what? After sending the wrong fixtures up here, he sent the ones we should have received to Sierra Vista. That's a town many miles below Tucson and a heck of a long way from Phoenix.

"The guy in charge called the truck driver on his cell and told him to turn around and come back with the stuff I needed. I forgot to take my cell with me, by the way. I waited and waited and waited, and the driver didn't show. So I had the supplier call him again and it turned out the radiator blew on his truck and he was stranded along the highway.

"So, the boss says for me to sit tight and he'd send another truck to get the fixtures off the broken truck and bring them back to Tucson for me.

"But, Joey?" Mark said, tilting Joey's chin up with one finger so their eyes met. "I decided right there on the spot that you were more important than bathroom fixtures. I knew you'd be watching for me and even if I called and said I was going to be way late, you would worry. So, I told the boss of the supply place to get those fixtures to me the minute he could, but I was leaving because I had a special little boy waiting for me to come home."

"Really?" Joey said. "You said that?"

"I did," Mark said, smiling. "I drove straight here as fast as I could, without breaking the speed-limit laws, of course. I didn't even stop to eat and I think my stomach caved in because it's so empty. But, hey, buddy, I love you, and there hasn't been a bathroom fixture made, or a construction schedule put on paper, that is more important to me than you are. I know that now, Joey. I swear to you that I do. Okay?"

"Okay," Joey yelled, and flung his arms around Mark's neck again.

Cedar got to her feet as two tears spilled onto her cheeks. "I'm sorry I was so harsh," she said, dashing the tears away. "Oh, Mark, I…" *Love you so much. So very much.* "…I'll fix you a sandwich."

Cedar hurried from the room, terrified that her true feelings for Mark Chandler would come tumbling out of her mouth.

Mark understood now, she thought, as she yanked food out of the refrigerator. Oh, he was going to be such a wonderful father to Joey. During the hours Mark was away, he'd reexamined his priorities and realized that Joey was so much more important than money in the bank for the future. Joey needed him *now* and Mark knew that.

Cedar jerked in surprise as she felt Mark's hands on her shoulders as she stood at the counter constructing his sandwich.

"Hey," he said, "why the tears?"

"I was just very moved by what you said. You understand that Joey…oh, never mind. You don't need me to tell you what you understand. You're here and that says it all."

Mark turned her to face him.

"I'm a little slow on the uptake at times, Cedar, but I usually come out of the ether eventually. Let's just say that I shifted my priorities today. When Joey lost his parents, I lost my sister and I miss her like hell. I need that kiddo to trust me, believe in me. I need him to love me, and I intend to earn that love.

I'm his father now and I don't take that title lightly. Thanks to you and what you've been hammering at me, I finally woke up."

Cedar nodded, unable to speak as fresh tears misted her eyes.

"And, Cedar?" Mark said, his voice husky with emotion. "I need you, too." *And I love you so damn much.* "I really do."

He kissed her deeply, delving his tongue into the sweet darkness of her mouth as her fingers inched into his hair.

The kiss was heat. Passions soaring to greet the sparkling diamond stars in the sky and nudge the moon from its hiding place.

The kiss was words. Declarations of irrevocable love tucked in secret chambers of hearts, afraid to be spoken.

The kiss was theirs. And they savored every wondrous, sensuous second of it.

"Yes!" Joey yelled, causing them to step quickly away from each other.

Acutely aware of his arousal, Mark looked over his shoulder at Joey rather than turn to face him. Joey had pulled Puncho into the kitchen and gave the clown a smothering hug.

"Yes! Yes! Yes!" Joey hollered, punching his fists in the air. "You're doing the kissing stuff. That means you're gonna do the loving stuff, and you can do the getting married stuff, and Cedar can live with us just like I said and—"

"Oh, good Lord," Cedar whispered.

"Whoa, whoa, whoa," Mark said, finally able to turn and stride across the room to Joey. "Hold it, Joey. Hey, isn't that the clown from Cedar's office? Wait, forget that part and listen to me, buddy. Just because a man and woman kiss each other doesn't mean—"

"Yes!" Joey said, jumping up and down.

Mark placed a hand on Joey's head to stop his imitation of a pogo stick.

"That's better," Mark said, keeping his hand on Joey's head. "Now. Listen. Just because a man and woman kiss each other, it doesn't mean they are in love."

"Yes, it does," Joey said, folding his arms over his chest. "My mom and dad kissed bunches of times and they loved each other and were married for years and years before they…before they became angels. So I know about this stuff. You love Cedar."

Got it in one, sport, Mark thought, dropping his hand from Joey's head. But the lady isn't interested in love and marriage, so…

"Cedar can live with us now, Uncle Mark," Joey said. "Right?"

"Wrong," Mark said. "Cedar is going to buy a different house for her and Oreo. She's going to live there and we're going to live…where we live. End of story."

Ends of stories could be rewritten, Cedar thought, staring at the scene before her. She blinked and shook her head. Finish making the man's sandwich, for Pete's sake, because his stomach is caving in. She spun around and began to slap whatever she could find on onto the bread. Now, knock off the daydreaming nonsense—again—and slap some mustard on this mess.

"Just because you're a grown-up," Joey said, "doesn't mean you're right all the time, Uncle Mark."

"Um, Cedar?" Mark said, commanding her attention. "Could you help me out here?"

Cedar sighed. She carried a plate with Mark's sandwich, as well as a glass of milk to the table. "Mark, sit down and get this food into your caved-in stomach," she said.

"Joey, you're absolutely correct in saying that grown-ups are not right all the time just because they're adults. However, there are some things that you have to be a grown-up to really understand. Love between a man and woman, the getting-married kind of love, is one of those things."

"But…" Joey started.

"No, honey," Cedar continued, "we're not going to discuss this further tonight. It's past your bedtime and you're very tired. Your Uncle Mark is going to eat his sandwich, then take you and Puncho home and tuck you into bed." She smiled. "Although I think it would be best to have Puncho stand next to your bed, not actually try to share it with you."

Joey laughed. "He'd take up all the space in my bed and he doesn't even have any jammies."

"That's true," Cedar said, then looked at Mark. "By the way, Mark, *this* Puncho is Joey's to keep forever. We went to the mall today and got him."

"Cool," Mark said. "Thanks for the rescue, too."

"What rescue?" Joey said.

"Figure of speech," Mark said, then took a bite of his sandwich. He lifted the edge of the top piece of bread and peered under it. "Interesting."

"Oh?" Cedar said, raising one eyebrow.

"But delicious," Mark said quickly. "Great sandwich. Top-notch. Best sandwich I've had…all day. Thank you very much for fixing it for me."

Joey yawned.

"Come on, my sleepy friend," Cedar said, extending a hand toward the little boy. "You can stretch out on the bed in my guest room while Uncle Mark eats his fantastic sandwich and has some cookies or something for dessert."

"'Kay," Joey said. Yawning again, he wrapped an arm around Puncho's neck and dragged the clown with them as they left the kitchen.

In the guest room, Cedar removed Joey's shoes, watched as he settled onto the bed, then covered him with an afghan she'd taken from the closet shelf. Joey fiddled with Puncho until the toy was exactly where he wanted it in relation to the bed.

"Close those great big dark eyes of yours," Cedar said, smiling. "Uncle Mark will carry you when he's ready to leave and you won't even have to wake up."

"Make sure Uncle Mark brings Puncho, too."

"I certainly will," Cedar said, then leaned over and kissed Joey on the forehead. She lingered there for a moment, inhaling his little-boy aroma. "Good night, Joey. I…"

Oh, I love you so much, Joey. And I love your Uncle Mark, too. But you were right. Just because I'm a grown-up doesn't mean I'm always right. And falling in love with Mark was really, really dumb.

"I enjoyed having you with me today," she finished.

"Yeah," Joey said, then his dark lashes drifted down.

Cedar gazed at him for another long moment,

then patted Puncho on the head and left the room, closing the door halfway.

She returned to the kitchen and sat down opposite Mark at the table as he picked up the second half of his sandwich.

"You really are a great shrinky-dink," Mark said, smiling slightly. "You defused an uncomfortable situation like the pro you are. Do you think he'll nail me again, though? You know, about you living with us because we kissed and, according to Joey, we are in love and can get married now?"

"I have no idea," Cedar said, plunking an elbow on the table and resting her chin in her palm. "He might, because he obviously wants the same kind of family unit that he had before. That's not unusual under the circumstances. He's like many of the children of divorce that I counsel. They hold on to the hope that their parents will get back together. Kids like and need consistency in their lives. Joey's world, as he knew it, was shattered and he's attempting to put it back together the way he wants it to be. He needs time and patience."

Mark nodded.

"I just want to say, Mark, that I respect you very much for realizing your priorities were off-kilter before."

"Yeah, well, I'll probably always worry about

whether or not I have enough money stashed away for the future, but I'll just have to live with that concern because I know now that Joey needs my undivided attention."

Cedar folded her hands on top of the table and frowned slightly. "Why are you so centered on the need for financial security, Mark? Hey, it's better than spending every dime you make and getting deeply in debt, but you're definitely on the opposite end of the pole."

"It's a long story," he said, then drained his glass.

"I'll listen if you want to share it."

"Who will listen?" he said, frowning. "Cedar the shrinky-dink, or Cedar the woman?"

"Cedar the woman," she said quietly.

Mark stared at her for a very long moment, then nodded slowly.

"Okay," he said finally. "Here it is. My father was an alcoholic. Big-time. He was fired from every job he had because of his drinking. My mother worked two jobs trying to keep food on the table and a roof over our heads. There was never enough money and I hate to tell you how many times my sister and I went to bed hungry."

"Oh, Mark, I'm so sorry."

"Yeah, well, that's how it was. When I was twelve and Mary was fourteen, my father got into yet another brawl at a bar when he was roaring drunk. He fell, hit his head, and died."

"Dear heaven," Cedar whispered.

"I got a paper route to help out. Mary babysat whenever she could. But even with my mother working two jobs and us contributing, we were continually evicted from shabby apartments because the rent wasn't paid. I made up my mind then," he said, his voice gritty, "that I would fix things, take care of my sister and mother, and never, ever go to bed hungry again. Focusing on that vow got me through high school.

"When I graduated, I went to work for a construction company and the owner took me under his wing and taught me every aspect of the trade. I was young, still making minimum wage, but I knew I had a future in the field that would enable me to provide my sister and mother with a decent home and allow my mom to stop working so hard."

Cedar nodded, her gaze riveted on Mark. She could hear the pain in his voice, saw it in his eyes as he shared the bleak memories of his childhood. She blinked back threatening tears.

"My sister married very young, but John was a good man. They moved to New York and she sent money to my mother whenever she could. Mary was safe and I knew she had enough to eat. I was still determined—driven, really—to make it possible for my mother to stop working, and have a nice house.

"When the owner of the construction company decided to retire, he allowed me to buy him out with installment payments. He was a helluva fine man. The father I never had. I renamed the business Chandler Construction and worked eighteen-hour days to make it bigger and better, still focused on doing right by my mother."

Mark stopped speaking. He pushed the crumbs from his sandwich around the plate, then drew a shuddering breath.

"But I didn't work hard enough or fast enough," he said, his voice choked with emotion. "My mother got pneumonia, and because she was so exhausted and in such poor health, she…she died."

Tears misted Cedar's eyes as she reached across the table to cover one of Mark's hands with her own.

"The years went by," Mark said, looking at their combined hands, "and I paid what I owed to my mentor, built myself a big house, put money in the bank and into a retirement portfolio. It was security for the future, but I couldn't forget the ghosts of the past, all the nights I went to bed hungry.

"Yeah, I wanted to get married, have kids, but I was always edgy, worried I didn't have enough money put aside. I'd wake up at night in a sweat, scared out of my mind that if I did marry and have children, something would happen and I wouldn't have the money to take care of things. I would be too late, too damn late to meet the needs of my family just as I'd been too late to save my mother."

Unnoticed tears spilled onto Cedar's cheeks.

"And there you have it," he said, meeting Cedar's gaze again. "The saga of Mark Chandler. Thanks to you, Cedar, I finally understand that Joey needs *me* now, more than he needs my money.

"Hell, I've got enough put away to put Joey through college twice. It will be tough for me to ease up on my work hours because it's the only life I've known for so damn long. But I'll get a handle on it...even though I'll probably *still* worry myself into a couple of ulcers because I'm not stashing as much away."

Mark reached over and drew a thumb through the trail of tears on Cedar's cheek. "Hey, I didn't mean to make you cry with my tale of woe," he said. "I thought you shrinky-dinks had tougher crusts than that because of what you deal with every day."

"But it was Cedar the woman who listened to you, Mark," she said, taking a trembling breath, "who is so very sorry you went through what you did, who knows that Joey is blessed to have you as a father."

The woman who loves you with every breath in my body. Loves you and your son.

"Even though I make gross scrambled eggs?" he said, producing a small smile.

"Even though," she said, nodding.

"Ah, Cedar, you've done so much for me, for Joey. I realize that he and I still have a long way to go, and we'll continue to need your help, but I want to thank you for all that you've given us. Don't say that it's all in a day's work because I sense—no, I know—it's more than that."

"Yes," she said softly, "it is."

Mark got to his feet and pulled gently on her hand so she would rise and meet him at the side of the table. He looked at her questioningly and she answered by stepping close to him, freeing her hand, and encircling his neck with her arms.

He lowered his head and kissed her, lightly at first, then intensifying the pressure. A groan rumbled in Mark's chest. A whimper of desire caught in Cedar's throat.

Mark broke the kiss and spoke close to her lips. "I want you, Cedar. I want to make love with you so damn much."

"I want you, too, Mark."

"Joey?"

"He's sound asleep and Puncho is watching over him."

They went up the stairs to Cedar's bedroom, their

pace quickening with each step as urgency engulfed them. In a hazy blur, they shed their clothes, Mark swept back the blankets on the bed, and they stretched out on the cool sheets, reaching instantly for each other.

Mark kissed Cedar deeply, causing hearts to beat with a wild tempo and heat to swirl, then tighten low in their bodies. They ended the kiss only long enough to take much-needed breaths, then Mark's mouth melted over Cedar's once again.

Mark finally broke the kiss to enable hands to roam, caress, explore. Lips followed where hands had been, suffusing them with a sense of awe as they savored the familiar that was somehow so gloriously new.

But they each knew that their true feelings, the love for the other that filled their hearts to overflowing, should not, could not, be declared aloud, as the spoken words might shatter the magical spell. They were simply Cedar and Mark existing in the moment, the now, not allowing the future to intrude.

When their desire reached a fever pitch, they joined bodies, becoming one, meshed into an entity that made it impossible to know where their separate beings began and ended.

They moved in a perfectly matched rhythm, rocking, holding fast, whispering the other's name. Heat consumed them as they soared, burning with exquisite pain that carried them up and up, then flung them into oblivion seconds apart.

"Mark!"

"My Cedar."

The cool sheets beckoned them to return and they did so reluctantly. Mark shifted off Cedar and she nestled close, resting one hand on the moist curls on his muscled chest, feeling his heart returning to a normal beat beneath her palm.

I love you, Cedar, Mark thought.

Oh, Mark, how I love you, Cedar's mind hummed.

As they began to drift off to sleep, Mark forced himself to release his hold and sit up on the edge of the bed.

"Mark?"

"If I sleep now, I'll be out for the night," he said, looking at her over his shoulder. "It's been a long, exhausting day. I can't be here in the morning because Joey will think he was right and we were wrong, and we're all going to live together. Get the drift?"

Cedar nodded.

"I hate to make you get up, but I want you to lock the door behind me when I carry Joey out."

"Yes, of course," she said, slipping from the bed

and reaching for her clothes. "And Puncho. You mustn't forget Puncho." She paused. "I wish…well, I wish you could stay."

"Oh, lady," he said, chuckling, "so do I, believe me."

Soon, much too soon, they were at the front door, a sleeping Joey propped against Mark's shoulder, Puncho tucked under his other arm. Mark kissed Cedar, then she held the door open for him so he could maneuver his cargo through.

"Thank you," he said, turning to look at her from the porch. "I…well…thank you."

Cedar smiled. "Good night, Mark."

She stood in the doorway until she could no longer see the lights of Mark's truck as they disappeared into the darkness. She closed and locked the door, then slid down to the floor, her arms wrapped around her knees, and wept.

She cried because she was deeply in love with a magnificent man but couldn't tell him because she couldn't bear the thought of his rejection if he knew she—no, she couldn't even bear to dwell on her secret because it hurt too much.

She cried because she loved Joey, too, but she'd never be his mother because she would never be Mark's wife.

She cried because hovering within her was the

chilling fear that Cindy might change her mind about allowing Cedar to adopt her baby and that dream would be destroyed, too.

She cried for all that was just beyond her reach, and suddenly she felt so very, very lonely.

She cried until she had no more tears to shed.

Chapter Ten

Cedar was in the middle of a stress-induced cleaning-of-the-house frenzy the next afternoon when the telephone rang.

"Hello, darling," her mother said when Cedar answered. "How are you?"

You don't want to know, Cedar thought miserably. "Fine, just fine," she said, forcing cheerfulness into her tone. "How are you? And Dad?"

"Well, we're having second thoughts about going on the cruise at Christmas with the other couples we planned the trip with."

"Why?" Cedar said, carrying the portable telephone into the living room so she could settle on the sofa. "That's your dream vacation, Mother. What's the problem?"

"We just hate the thought of your being alone during the holidays," Joyce said. "Our departure date is getting closer. As it does, we keep picturing you having a bleak time all alone."

"Don't you dare cancel that trip because of me," Cedar said, sitting up straighter on the sofa. "Thanksgiving went by without me even noticing because I'm so busy. Plus you know from past years that I need to be here at Christmas in case my clients experience any crises. Last year I didn't fly down to see you until several days after Christmas, remember?"

"Yes, yes, but still—"

"Mother, you and Dad are going on that cruise," Cedar said firmly. "I have so much going on right now, I'm not even certain I could get to Florida until after the new year.

"I've decided to put this house on the market and get something new that isn't a money pit." Cedar laughed. "Dad will love the chance to say I told you so.

"My practice is growing beyond my wildest

hopes and my days are so full and—have I convinced you yet that you're worrying for nothing? I'll be just fine through the holidays. They'll zoom by. Okay?"

"Well, if you're certain that—"

"I am. Have you gone shopping for wonderful clothes to take on the trip?"

"As a matter of fact, I did go on a spree with two of the other women who are going on the cruise. Oh, my, we found some lovely things. There's one dress, Cedar, that is scrumptious. It's…"

Cedar managed to comment in all the right places as her mother chattered on. A part of her mind, though, was carrying on a mental dialogue with her mother that she knew she couldn't say aloud.

Mom, I'm in love with a fantastic man. His name is Mark Chandler and I've lost my heart to him and don't know how to get it back. He doesn't know that I love him because there's no point in telling him. I don't know how he feels about me, and even if, by some miracle, he is in love with me, he would back away if he knew my secret.

And there's Joey. Oh, you should see Joey, Mother. He's seven years old and so sweet. His parents were killed in an accident and Mark is his guardian. I'm helping Joey deal with his pain and I've come to love that little boy, too.

As if that wasn't enough on my emotional plate I might be adopting a baby girl. Can you believe that, Mom? Me, a mother? I'm not going to tell you because I don't want you to be disappointed if Cindy changes her mind. I won't believe it's really true until Cindy has the baby, signs the papers, and I'm holding my daughter in my arms.

So, you see, it's better this way, your going away for the holidays because I'd probably burst into tears the moment I saw you and Dad, and spill the beans about everything and that would never do.

"You will, won't you?" Joyce said.

"Um…"

"Keep us up to date on your doings?"

"Oh. Yes, of course, I always do, you know that. I'll talk to you again before you leave on your trip. Oops, there's my kitchen timer ringing. I have a chocolate cake in the oven. Gotta go. Love you. Tell Dad I love him. 'Bye for now."

"Goodbye, darling," Joyce said.

Cedar's shoulders slumped as she pressed the off button on the phone. She wished she really did have a chocolate cake in the oven. A chocolate binge might perk up her gloomy mood, she thought, leaning her head on the top of the sofa. Goodness, she was feeling sorry for herself today.

Christmas would be here before she knew it, and

she hadn't even thought about gifts for her parents and Bethany and—

Cedar sighed.

Wouldn't it be fun to shop for Joey? And she'd spend delicious hours going from store to store to find the perfect gift for Mark. As presents to herself, she'd buy baby things: soft, cuddly sleepers, blankets, a little dress with matching booties, sweater and bonnet. And wallpaper. Bunny wallpaper for the nursery.

"Keep this up," Cedar said, getting to her feet, "and you'll end up baking that chocolate cake and eating the whole thing yourself."

She'd decided to return to her cleaning frenzy when the doorbell rang. She marched to the front door and flung it open.

"Oh," she said, surprised. "Moose. Hi. Come in."

"I should have called first," Moose said, entering the house, "but I took a chance that you might be home. I'd like to talk to you, Cedar."

"Sure. Let's go into the living room."

Moose settled his enormous self onto the sofa and Cedar sat opposite him in an easy chair.

"Would you care for something to drink?" she asked.

"No, no," Moose said. "Thanks. Listen, it's about this house."

Cedar sighed. "The one that's falling apart."

"It's a super house," Moose said, smiling. "I was talking to three of my buddies about it. We'd love to restore this baby to what it once was. There is so much potential and we have the skills to do the job and turn this house around for a nice profit. Would you consider selling it to us?"

"Oh. Well. Goodness. I mean, sure, Moose."

"Would whatever it's appraised at be a fair price for you?"

"It wouldn't be fair to *you*," Cedar said. "An appraiser wouldn't know all the things that are just waiting to go wrong."

"We'll pay the appraisal figure," Moose said, "and we won't rush you to move because we know you have to figure out where you want to live. How's that?"

Cedar narrowed her eyes. "Are you my fairy godfather in a great big body?"

"There you go," Moose said, laughing. "My wife will love that description of me. Do we have a deal?"

"Oh, yes, we certainly do," Cedar said. "I think you and your friends are cuckoo, but I'm not about to argue with you."

Moose got to his feet. "I'll have the papers drawn up. We'll pay for the appraisal, too, so don't worry about that." He paused. "Mark said you were looking at those new homes we're building close to here."

"Well, yes, I went and took a look at them," she said, rising.

"You can't go wrong buying a place built by Chandler Construction," Moose said. "Did you see a model you really liked?"

The big one, Cedar thought. The one that had room for her, Mark, Joey, the new baby girl, Oreo and even a dog. Yep, that was a dandy house.

"I'm still mulling," she said.

Moose started toward the front door. "My wife is into mulling. She says women need to think things through more than men do. I'll agree with that one. Women are very complicated creatures."

"No, we're not," Cedar said, laughing. "We make perfect sense to ourselves...most of the time. Well, what can I say to you, Moose, but thank you."

"No, we thank you," he said, opening the front door. "My buddies and I are going to get a real kick out of this project." He paused. "So, um, I guess you're seeing quite a bit of Mark these days. You know, because you're helping Joey and...Mark says you're doing a terrific job with that little dude. Yep, Mark says a lot of great things about you, Cedar. He smiles more lately, too. How about you, Cedar? Are you smiling because you and Mark...what I mean is...ah, heck, I'm not doing a very good job of this."

"No, you're not," Cedar said, smiling. "Just chalk

it up to another one of those things that complicated women do better than men."

"Aren't you even going to give me a hint as to whether or not something is going on with you and Mark?"

"No."

"Oh, well, I tried. Glad we could at least do business about the house," Moose said, grinning. "I'll be in touch soon about that. See ya."

"See ya," she said, then closed the door behind him.

As she wandered back into the living room, her mind was racing. She'd sold this monster of a house, she thought incredulously. She could get something new and sparkly that would not fall down around her ears. A house big enough for—

Oreo strolled into the room.

Big enough for her and her cat, she thought dismally, because that was exactly how it could end up. Just single Cedar and her fat cat. Oh, she was definitely going to bake a chocolate cake.

On Monday morning, Cedar had no sooner greeted Bethany and entered her office when her secretary buzzed her on the intercom.

"Yes?" Cedar said, pressing the button on the small box on the desk.

"Your social-worker friend Kathy is on the phone

for you, Cedar," Bethany said. "She said you're expecting to hear from her this morning."

"I...yes, I am. Thank you."

Cedar sank gratefully into the chair behind her desk, her legs suddenly trembling. She pressed one hand to her forehead for a moment, then reached for the telephone receiver, ignoring the fact that her hand was not the least bit steady.

"Kathy?" Cedar said.

"Good morning, Cedar," Kathy said cheerfully. "Well, are congratulations in order? Are you a mommy-to-be?"

"Oh, Kathy." Cedar propped an elbow on top of the desk and rested her forehead in her palm. "I want that baby girl so badly. But I'm terrified that I'll allow myself to get excited about being a mother, only to end up bitterly heartbroken again and—"

"Again?"

Cedar's eyes widened and she sat bolt upward. "What I mean is," she said, scrambling for what to say, "is that I've had...yes, I've had heartache in the past. You know, I told you I'm divorced and...anyway, what if I put things in motion to adopt Cindy's baby and she changes her mind at the last minute? I couldn't bear it."

"I understand your fears, Cedar. I've done so many of these adoptions and there have been times when I cautioned the people expecting to adopt the baby to be prepared for anything because I wasn't that convinced that the decision made by the pregnant gal was that solid.

"I've developed an instinct about these situations, Cedar, and I haven't been wrong in years. This deal with Cindy is good to go. She wants to return home, to be fifteen years old again. She's adamant, though, that you are the only one she'll allow to adopt her baby."

"Mmm," Cedar said, for lack of a better response.

"This is what we call a 'good' baby, too. It's a term we use when there've been no drugs, no alcohol abuse, and the mom has had ongoing prenatal care.

"Cedar, I spoke with Cindy's mother last night. She said that if all goes as Cindy hopes, they'll move out of Arizona once you adopt the baby so Cindy can have a fresh start in a high school where no one knows she was a pregnant teen. So, my friend, what's the verdict?"

Cedar drew a steadying breath, looked heavenward for a moment, then squared her shoulders. "Yes," she said, then felt a smile begin to form on her lips. "Yes, Kathy, I want to adopt Cindy's baby. I want to be a mother and—yes."

"Fantastic! Oh, I'm so thrilled for you. I've got

first dibs on giving you a baby shower. Won't that be fun? I love to shop for baby things as long as I'm not the one who's going to use them. Like diapers. Ick."

"Now wait a minute, Kathy," Cedar said. "I trust your instincts about these things, I do, but I'm still scared it won't really happen. I can't help it. So, I don't want anyone to know about this until it's a done deal and…until I'm more settled about this in my mind. Promise?"

"Darn. Well, okay, tell me when you're settled, then I'll put on a bash for you. Hey, the baby is due around Valentine's Day. You can name her Cupid. How's that?"

"To quote you…ick," Cedar said, laughing.

"You're right. Anyway, these young girls have a tendency to deliver early."

"I have to buy a new house because I've found a buyer for my monster."

"Get to it. That little girl will be here before you know it. Well, I promised to call Cindy at her foster home after I spoke to you, so I'd better go. She'll know the scoop when you see her this afternoon at her appointment. She's going to be one happy camper.

"Oh, before I forget, I'm going to put through the paperwork to have today's session with Cindy be the last one. You did a super job with her as far as making her do a reality check. Thank goodness she made the right decisions for herself, the baby and...hey, you. Well, I'm gone. 'Bye, Cedar. I really am excited for you."

"Thank you, Kathy, for everything. 'Bye for now."

Cedar replaced the receiver, then pressed her hands to her flushed cheeks, before moving them down to cover her racing heart. In the next instant, she got to her feet, unable to sit still for another second and began to pace around the office, thoughts tumbling through her mind one after another.

She was going to do it, she thought incredulously. Oh, dear God, she was going to be a mother. Have a daughter. A precious little girl. That dream had been shattered years ago and now she wanted to dash to the outer office and tell Bethany the glorious news, share it with her parents, with Mark and Joey and Oreo and—

No, she had to keep silent. She just had to. Despite Kathy's reassurances, she feared that something would go wrong...again. That all her hopes and dreams, her incredible joy would be smashed to smithereens...again.

She was going to be emotionally demolished if the adoption fell through, whether she kept it a secret or not. She wasn't making much sense keeping the baby to herself, she supposed, but that was the way it was going to be.

"Cupid?" Cedar said, allowing herself to smile. "No, I don't think so. I'll make a list of names and…"

Her smile faded.

No, there would be no list of names. Not yet. That made the baby too real, too…hers. No, no names on a list. Not yet.

A knock at the door brought Cedar from her tangled thoughts. A moment later, her secretary opened the door and poked her head in.

"You're due in court, Cedar," Bethany said. "Oh, and since you've been spacey ever since those gorgeous flowers arrived way back when, I'll remind you that this afternoon you have appointments with Cindy, then Joey. You'd probably come back down to earth if you told me who sent those roses."

"Cindy," Cedar said.

"Oh, and do you have a bridge you want to sell me?" Bethany said. "Cindy did *not* send you those roses."

"No, no, of course she didn't," Cedar said.

Kathy was going to call Cindy and tell her that Cedar had agreed to adopt her baby. Cindy was liable to babble the bulletin to Bethany and—oh, good grief.

"Bethany, take the afternoon off."

"I beg your pardon?"

"I mean it. Don't you have Christmas shopping to do? I only have the two clients after lunch. You can have the service pick up any calls, and I'll check with them after Joey's appointment.

"View it as a fact-finding mission. You can tell me where the bargains are before I shop for gifts."

"Well, if you put it that way," Bethany said, "how can I refuse?"

"Exactly. You're a gem. Now, I'm off to court. I'll grab a bite while I'm out and be back in time to meet Cindy. See you tomorrow. Bye."

"You're acting weird," Bethany said, narrowing her eyes. "Why are you shuffling me off to the mall when Cindy, then Joey are expected to arrive here? Joey…and his Uncle Mark."

"I…"

"Yes!" Bethany punched a fist in the air. "I did it. I'm Magnum, P.I., and Columbo rolled into one. You're afraid I'll pick up on the vibes between you and Mark Chandler. Uncle Mark sent the roses." She beamed. "Darn, I'm good. And, oh, that Mark is so yummy."

Cedar snatched up her briefcase and marched past a grinning Bethany.

"I'm taking the Fifth," Cedar said, as she zoomed by.

"What that Mark does for a pair of faded jeans is to die for," Bethany said wistfully.

"Aakk," Cedar yelled, then slammed the door to the suite behind her as she left.

"Will you be in the room with me when I deliver the…your baby?" Cindy said. "I saw this thing on TV once where the people who were adopting the baby were in the delivery room and cut the cord. That is so gross…but, anyway, I'd really like you to be there."

"What about your mother?" Cedar asked.

"No, my mom doesn't want to see the baby. I know it's her granddaughter and all, but she said it would be better to just put this behind us. We're going to move to California, which is so cool I can hardly wait."

"I'm glad you're excited about the move." Cedar smiled at the teenager.

"Oh, I am," Cindy said. "Anyway, my mom said she'd be okay with me calling you when I go into labor. I wish I didn't have to do that labor junk because we're talking major pain here. So…will you be there to see your baby born?"

"I…well, I…yes," Cedar said, feeling an achy sensation in her throat. "Thank you for asking me. And, Cindy? Thank you for trusting me with this precious gift. I'll be the very best mother I can be."

"I know. That's why I picked you. Are we done? I'm hungry."

Cedar glanced at the clock on the wall.

"Yes, our time is up." She got to her feet and came around the desk to hug Cindy after the teenager heaved herself up. "Thank you from the bottom of my heart."

"Sure," Cindy said, patting Cedar on the back. "I'm going to learn to surf. Cool, huh?"

"Way cool," Cedar said, blinking back threatening tears.

"'Bye for now," Cindy said, heading for the door. "See you when I'm doing my screaming and yelling thing. Remember that you're supposed to cut the cord. Oh, that is just so majorly gross."

Cindy wasn't going to change her mind, Cedar thought frantically, after the girl closed the door behind her. Anyone listening to Cindy would know that she had already moved on. She was going to learn how to surf, for heaven's sake.

It was really going to happen. She was going to be a mother. It *was* going to happen.

Wasn't it?

"Have faith," Cedar whispered, closing her eyes. "Believe in what you just heard Cindy say. Come on, Cedar, have some faith."

Chapter Eleven

Faith.

Cedar opened her eyes, then smiled.

"Faith. Oh, yes, it's perfect. I'm going to name my daughter Faith Cedar Kennedy. Faith."

She stared into space and repeated the name over and over like a mantra, ignoring the fact that she'd given herself a firm directive not to make a list of names for the baby, let alone pick one.

She blinked suddenly, looked at the clock and realized that Joey and Mark would be arriving at any moment for Joey's appointment.

She rushed into the small bathroom and gazed at her reflection in the mirror to be certain she didn't look any different, that there wasn't a telltale clue that she was maybe, oh, please, yes, going to be a mother in a handful of weeks.

"You're acting like a dolt," she told her image.

After marching to the outer office, she plunked down in Bethany's chair so she'd be prepared to give Joey his snack. Moments later, the door opened and Joey and Mark entered, Mark attempting to brush dust from his jeans as he walked.

Bethany was right, Cedar thought dreamily, staring at Mark. What that man did for a pair of faded jeans was...

"Hi, Cedar," Joey said, from where he stood in front of the desk.

"What?" she said, shifting her gaze to the little boy. "Oh. Hi, Joey. Want to pick a juice box from the refrigerator and a granola bar from the basket?"

"Sure," Joey said, heading toward the treats.

"Sure...what?" Mark said.

"Huh?" Joey said. "Oh, sure and thank you."

"You're welcome," Cedar said, smiling.

"Well, this brings back memories," Mark said, moving into the space in front of the desk that Joey had vacated. "I do believe that the first time we met you were impersonating Bethany and I made a total and complete jerk of myself."

Cedar laughed. "Yes, indeed, your memory serves you correctly, sir." She paused, her smile fading. "A great deal has happened since that day."

Mark slid his hands into the back pockets of his jeans and nodded. "Yes," he said quietly, "that's very true. A lot has changed, hasn't it?" *And at the top of the list, Cedar Kennedy, is the fact that I've fallen in love with you. How's that for stupid, Ms. Shrinky-dink, considering that you don't want any part of hearth, home, marriage and kids?* "For example, I learned how to make barbecue chicken."

And I learned how to love again, Cedar thought, and fell in love with you, Mark Chandler. Some shrinky-dink I am. I lost control of my own emotions.

"Cedar, I—"

"Would you like a snack, Mark?" Cedar said, cutting him off as she got to her feet.

"No, thanks."

"Joey," Cedar said, pulling her gaze from Mark, "are you about finished with your goodies?"

"Yep," he said, throwing the empty juice box and granola bar wrapper in the trash basket. "All done."

"Okay," Cedar said, walking around the desk. "Let's go into my office. Mark, will you join us, please?"

"Me?" he said. "Well, okay."

In her office, Cedar settled into the chair behind her desk and waved Joey and Mark into the chairs opposite her.

"We need to chat about Christmas," she said finally, looking at Mark, then Joey. "It will be here very soon, and I'm sure you've noticed that decorations are already up in the stores and that Santa even made some early appearances during the parades on Thanksgiving."

"I used to believe in Santa Claus when I was a little kid," Joey said, "but now I'm big and I know Santa is really my..." He stopped speaking and frowned. "I don't want to talk about Christmas stuff." He crossed his arms tightly on his chest. "No."

"Okay," Cedar said. "Mark, why don't you share some of your Christmas traditions with us?"

"Traditions?" Mark said. "Like what? Give me a hint here."

"Well, I assume you put up a tree in your living room and decorate it," Cedar said.

"No," Mark said slowly, "I don't."

"Why not?" Cedar said pleasantly.

"It's more like...why?" he said. "I mean, I'm there all alone, so what's the point? I don't even own any decorations for a tree, or doodads to put around the house during the holidays. I just treat Christmas like any other day off from work. I sleep late and watch some football." He shrugged. "No tree, no traditions."

"Well, that's not very nice," Joey yelled, which caused Mark to snap his head around and stare at the boy in shock. "I don't want to sleep late and watch dumb football on Christmas. Aren't we going to have a tree and a bunch of presents and stuff? What kind of person are you? You're like that green Grinch guy, that's what you are."

"Now, Joey," Cedar said calmly, "let's be fair. Uncle Mark didn't have a family here in Phoenix before, and sometimes when people live alone they don't do all the usual Christmasy things. But now he has you and that changes everything. However, he doesn't have any experience at doing this, so maybe you could help him out. What do you think?"

"Well, maybe," Joey said. "Yeah, I guess so."

"That would very generous of you. Right, Mark?"

"Huh? Oh. Yes, that's…swell. Thanks, buddy, I appreciate your being willing to lend me a hand."

"You're going to need lots of stuff, Uncle Mark. Tons. Maybe we should make a list, you know? And you can't forget presents. Presents are very, very 'portant."

Mark chuckled. "You betcha."

"How's this for a plan, Joey?" Cedar said. "We'll

skip your Wednesday appointment, because the three of us will go out for pizza Friday night, then to the mall to start getting the tons of stuff Uncle Mark needs."

"Cool," Joey said.

"Mark?"

"Cool," Mark said.

"Super," Cedar said. "Joey, I need to speak to Uncle Mark alone, so you may color in the books in the outer office."

"'Kay," Joey said, sliding off the chair then running from the room.

"Damn, you're good," Mark said, shaking his head. "You turned Joey around on the subject of Christmas so smoothly, it was awesome. Very slick."

"The reason I want to go along on the shopping expedition is because something might trigger a memory of Christmases Joey spent with his parents and he's liable to have a meltdown in the middle of the mall. I need to be there in case that happens."

Mark smiled. "Are you sure you want to be seen in the company of the green Grinch guy?"

"I'll suffer through it," she said, matching his smile. The next moment she frowned. "I guess you didn't ship any Christmas things from your sister's house to yours?"

"No, I blew that, huh? I donated the Christmas

decorations, along with a lot of other stuff to a charity thrift shop. I suppose it would be better if Joey had things he recognized from past holidays, but...damn."

"Don't be so hard on yourself, Mark. You were under tremendous stress when you made those decisions. Besides, this might be better. You and Joey will create new memories. And you'll pick out Christmas doodads and ornaments together."

"Thanks for letting me off the hook on that one, Cedar. Hey, I'd like to hire a sitter for Joey and take you out again, just the two of us. What do you say? Could we do that soon?"

"Well, yes," she said, averting her gaze from Mark's. "Soon."

"When?"

"Let's see how Joey does Friday night, shall we? If he falls apart, he'll need you to stick close for a while. There's no way to predict how he'll do during the holidays. It's all wait and watch."

"I get the drift." Mark paused. "What are you doing for Christmas?"

"I don't...really have...any plans," Cedar said, straightening some papers on her desk that didn't need straightening. "My parents are going on a cruise, but I prefer to stay in Phoenix, because Christmas is a difficult time for some of my clients."

"Oh. Well, how about spending Christmas day with me and Joey? Just don't expect me to prepare a turkey dinner. I could whip up barbecue chicken, though. I'm getting to be a real pro at that one."

"Oh, I don't know, Mark. You and Joey need to establish some traditions that belong to just the two of you."

"Okay," he said, nodding. "We'll start a tradition of inviting someone over on Christmas to share the day with us. How's that?"

"I give up," Cedar said, laughing. "Yes, thank you, I'd be delighted to spend Christmas day with you and Joey."

"Good. That's good." Mark nodded. "Hey, Moose told me that he and some buddies of his are going to buy your house."

"Yes, I was stunned and grateful. Now I have to settle on where I want to go, how large a house I want, and on and on. I want a fenced-in backyard with a tree for shade, and I'd like to be fairly close to an elementary school so that…" Cedar stopped speaking, hoping that Mark hadn't really picked up on the last of what she said. "I just have a great many decisions to make fairly quickly, that's all."

"Back up," Mark said, frowning. "Why do you want to be close to an elementary school? Is Oreo the wonder cat going to enroll?"

So much for wishful thinking, Cedar thought.

"I read somewhere," she said, scrambling for an explanation for her slip of the tongue, "that being near a good elementary school increases the resale value of your home." Not bad, she thought, considering she was winging it. "Yes, that's what I read."

"That's a matter of opinion," Mark said. "Anyway, you haven't even bought a house yet, so why discuss selling it?"

"You're right," Cedar said.

"Moose said he's in no hurry to close the deal and told you to take your time deciding what you want to buy," Mark said. "That's good advice, Cedar. Don't rush. Take it slow and easy."

And maybe, he thought, lightning would strike and Cedar would realize that she was in love with him, wanted to spend the rest of her life with him and would move into the huge house he already owned. Right. And maybe he'd win the lottery and become an instant millionaire. Hell.

"Why are you frowning like that?" Cedar said.

"I'm hungry," Mark said. "I frown a lot when I'm hungry."

"Well, our session is over for today, so—oh, wait, there's one other thing. Are you aware that schools close for the holidays? There's no reason for you to know that as I doubt they've sent a note home from school with Joey yet. I just thought I'd mention it. I suppose he'll have to spend those days at day care because you'll be working."

"I've already covered it," Mark said. "Joey will go to day care in the morning, I'll knock off at noon, then we'll have the rest of the day together. Between Moose and Jeff as my foremen, all of Chandler Construction's jobs will be covered and I'll be available in case of an emergency."

Cedar leaned forward. "You're going to work half days during Joey's entire break from school?"

"Yep," Mark said. "I told you that I finally understand that some things are more important than working 'til I drop so I can salt money away. It will cost me bucks to pay Moose and Jeff extra to pick up the slack for my not being there, but so be it. Joey needs a father more than I need the money."

"You're wonderful," Cedar said, awe ringing in her voice. She blinked. "What I mean is, *that's* wonderful. It's an especially beneficial schedule because of Joey's emotional state at that time."

Mark frowned. "You're doing your shrinky-dink thing, Cedar."

"I know," she said, sighing. "Ignore that last part. Just know that I think you're…well, you're a very special man for what you're doing for Joey. Very special." She cleared her throat. "I'll drive to your house on Friday night and we'll leave from there for pizza and the shopping spree. Does six o'clock suit you?"

"That's fine," Mark said, getting to his feet at the same time as Cedar. "And give some thought to us going out for the evening alone, okay? I know, I know, it depends on Joey's emotional state, but at least think about it."

"I will."

"If you'd like me to check over a house you're considering buying, I'd be glad to do that for you. Can't have you getting another monster to maintain," Mark said. And he could manage to slow things down considerably by finding a whole bunch of stuff wrong. "Yes, ma'am, I live to serve."

"That's very kind of you." Cedar smiled. "Of course, if I buy a house built by Chandler Construction, I won't have to worry about anything being defective. Will I?"

"No," Mark said, inwardly sighing. Damn.

"Well, until Friday night then. Have a good week."

"Why can't we see each other before then?" Mark said, wiggling his eyebrows.

Cedar laughed. "You look like Joey trying to con another cookie. I have a very busy week ahead, Mark."

"Well, hell, I tried." He started toward the door of

the office with Cedar following behind him. "You know, you might consider trying your own advice on for size." He stopped and turned to look at her. "I've cut back on my work hours because you made me understand that I was operating at an extreme level, but you're no slouch yourself in that department. You ever tally how many hours you put in during a given week, Cedar? Do you think maybe *you* ought to lighten up a tad? More than a tad even."

"I'm not the one who became an instant father," she said. But I'll definitely be cutting back on my work hours when I become a mother to Faith Cedar Kennedy. "There is that fact to consider, you know."

"Yeah, but I still think—"

"Uncle Mark?" Joey said, standing in the open doorway. "Are we done now? My stomach gobbled up the snack Cedar let me have and I'm hungry again."

"That's an amazing stomach you've got there, buddy," Mark said, laughing, "but I could use some food myself. Say goodbye to Cedar."

"'Bye."

"Goodbye, sweetie." Cedar smiled at Joey. "I'll see you Friday night."

"'Kay," Joey said. "I'll start the list of the tons of stuff we need."

"Cool," Cedar said.

"Way cool," Mark boomed, then winked at Cedar before he and Joey made their exit.

A heavy silence fell over the office and a shiver coursed through Cedar as she stood still, staring at the door that had closed behind Mark and Joey.

She loved them both so much, she thought. She loved Mark as a woman loves a man, and Joey as a mother loves a son. But they weren't hers to have. Not now. Not ever.

But, goodness, there was no reason to feel sorry for herself. She was going to be a mother, have a daughter to love. She and Faith and Oreo would be a family, a wondrous family.

But when Cedar started back toward her desk, she hesitated, then turned to look at the doorway one more time.

Chapter Twelve

When Cedar arrived at Mark's on Friday evening, she, Mark and Joey burst into laughter as they looked at one another. They were all wearing jeans and red sweaters.

"I thought I should look festive since we're on a Christmas mission tonight," Cedar said.

"That's where my head was, too," Mark said, grinning.

"This is so cool." Joey gave a happy giggle. "Like we're going to get our picture taken or something. A family photo op."

"Photo op?" Mark said, with another burst of laughter. "That's pretty high-tech jargon there, buddy."

"My friend, Robin, says her family always dresses the same for the picture for their Christmas cards and her dad calls it a family photo op. Since we all have red sweaters on, we could get a Christmas-card picture taken, too."

Out of the mouths of babes, Mark thought. But a family photo op wasn't in the cards for this trio.

"That wouldn't be possible, Joey," Cedar said.

"Why not?" Joey asked.

"Well…because Oreo isn't here wearing a red sweater," she answered quickly. "Now then, who's ready for pizza?"

"Me!" Joey shouted, the family portrait already forgotten. "I'm hungry. My stomach is caving in just like Uncle Mark's does when he's starving."

"Then let's rock and roll," Mark said.

Man, he thought, Cedar sure was good at whipping right out of any reference to all of them being a family. Oreo wasn't there in a red sweater? Geez.

They'd consumed an extra-large pizza with a multitude of toppings and a frosty pitcher of soda before arriving at the nearest mall to find a line of children waiting to sit on Santa's lap to whisper what they wanted on Christmas morning.

"You'd think Christmas was next week," Mark said, glancing around at the holiday decorations. "Look at the crowds already."

"Merchants stretch it out as long as possible," Cedar said, nodding. "It's no wonder that little kids think the big day will never arrive. They've been hyped for several weeks."

"Yep," Mark said, then shifted his gaze to Joey. "We didn't discuss a tree, Joey. I'd prefer to get an artificial one because real trees dry out fast here in Phoenix and are a fire hazard. That work for you?"

"'Kay." Joey shrugged. "Fake trees look as real as real trees. That's what my…my dad always said."

"He was a smart man, Joey," Cedar said, smiling at him warmly, "and you obviously take after him."

"Uncle Mark is smart, too," Joey said. "If he was a dumb-dumb, he wouldn't be able to build cool stuff. Are you going to get one of the houses Uncle Mark builds, Cedar?"

"I'm thinking it over," she said, "but right now let's concentrate on our assignment. Lights for the tree. Do you want all one color, or a lot of different kinds, like a rainbow?"

"A lot of colors," Joey said. "Now, this is 'portant. Some of the ornaments should be fancy glass ones, some should be wood, and some should be made by me out of paper. My mom said she liked mine best."

"I'm sure Cedar and I will like yours best, too, Joey," Mark said, ruffling the child's hair.

"Maybe," Joey muttered, staring at the toes of his shoes.

"Joey," Cedar said, hunkering down to look into his eyes, "if you're missing your mom and dad right now, that's perfectly understandable. If you decide at any point that you want to go home, then we'll go. You're in charge of this expedition, but it can be done a little bit at a time if that's easier for you."

Joey nodded slowly. "'Kay. I was getting really sad, but now I'm better because I'm the boss of the shopping. Let's get going."

Cedar rose and met Mark's gaze over the top of Joey's head.

"You saved the day again," Mark said. "You are so good at what you do, it must be very rewarding. I guess that's why you're focused on your career, instead of wanting a family of your own. Right?"

"No. Yes. No." Cedar threw up her hands. "Never mind."

"Come *on*," Joey said, tugging on Mark's hand.

Mark looked at Cedar for another long moment, then allowed Joey to lead him to a store with a twinkling Christmas tree in the front window. Cedar followed.

Inside the store, Mark picked up a plastic basket

and Joey began to place ornaments in it after giving each a careful scrutiny.

Cedar stopped in front of a small tree that had been decorated with a baby theme, ornaments printed with the words Baby's First Christmas, rattles, booties, teddy bears, tiny angels sleeping on a sliver of moon, ABC blocks and on and on.

She smiled as she looked from one ornament to the next, envisioning Faith, who would be old enough by next Christmas to be enchanted by the lights on the tree and the brightly colored packages beneath. The baby would no doubt be crawling by then, maybe even attempting to take her first steps, and would have to be watched every second to be certain she didn't treat herself to an early Christmas by tearing the wrappings from the presents.

These ornaments were darling, just exquisite, Cedar thought, as she looked at a sleeping baby with sugar plums and candy canes depicted above her head.

She was going to come back to this store on her own and buy some of these ornaments to tuck away for next year when Faith—no, that probably wasn't wise. She was getting ahead of herself again, just as she had when she settled on a name for her…for her daughter.

She had to stop this foolishness, she admonished

herself. Nothing was certain until Cindy signed those papers. So, don't think about the baby tonight, not tonight, she told herself. She was here for Joey. And for Mark.

Mark stood several feet away from Cedar, watching her intently as she looked at each and every one of the baby ornaments on the miniature tree.

Baby ornaments? His heart began to thunder in his chest as he looked at Cedar's flat stomach, then at the soft smile on her face. Hot damn, was Cedar pregnant with his baby? Was that why she was enthralled with the display?

He'd protected her when they'd made love, but those gizmos weren't one hundred percent perfect. Accidents happened. But, oh, man, if Cedar was carrying his child, it wouldn't be an accident. It would be a blessing, a…a fantastic gift.

They could be a real family, Cedar and him as husband and wife, father and mother, Joey their son, the baby their…daughter. Yes, a girl, a baby girl. Oh, yeah, and Cedar's weird cat that needed a red sweater.

Slow down, Chandler, he ordered himself. Just because Cedar was smiling at baby ornaments didn't mean she was pregnant, for crying out loud. He was getting carried away with—

Cedar splayed a hand on her stomach.

That cinched it, by damn. It was true. Cedar Kennedy was pregnant with his baby. Maybe. Oh, he hoped it was true. *Their* baby. This was wonderful, just—

"Uncle Mark?" Joey said, distracting Mark from his racing thoughts. "Are you listening to me?"

"Oh, sorry, sport. There's just so much to see in this store, it's hard to take it all in. What were you saying?"

"I like this wooden train ornament," Joey said, holding it high for Mark's inspection. "'Kay?"

"Sure. Plunk it right in the basket with the others. You're making some great choices."

"I know," Joey said, puffing out his chest. "I'm good at this stuff and—" He stopped speaking and walked slowly away.

"Joey?" Mark said.

Cedar came to Mark's side. "What's wrong, Mark?" she asked.

"I don't know," he said. "Joey was all jazzed up, then he suddenly went pale and headed toward that table over there. I'd better see what's going on."

"I'll come with you," she said, frowning.

When they reached Joey, Mark saw that he was staring at a display of snow globes. Joey's bottom lip was trembling and tears had slid onto his cheeks.

"Joey, honey?" Cedar said, bending over and

wrapping an arm around his shoulders. "What is it? What upset you, sweetheart?"

"My dad took me shopping for a Christmas present for my mom last year," he said, his voice trembling. "I picked a snow thing just like that." He pointed with a shaking finger. "The one with people skating on the ice. My mom…my mom said it was the best present she ever got, and she didn't pack it away with the Christmas stuff 'cause she wanted to see it every single day of the year and…" A sob caught in his throat.

"What a lovely memory," Cedar said gently. "I know you feel sad right now, Joey, but if you think about it, it's one of those special moments to tuck away in your heart." She paused. "You know, it might be nice to have that snow globe in your bedroom. Not to make you sad when you look at it, but to remember how happy your mother was when you gave it to her. What do you think?"

"I wouldn't have to pack it away with the Christmas stuff?" Joey said, with a little hiccup.

"Not if you didn't want to," Cedar said.

Joey looked up at Mark.

"It's up to you," Mark said. "Whatever you decide is fine with me."

"But it costs bunches of money," Joey said.

"That's not important," Mark said. "What matters

is you. Remember, Joey, your mother was my sister and I miss her, too. We could both look at the globe whenever we felt like it and smile because we'd know she was so happy when you gave it to her. What do you say?"

"Well…" Joey said, then sniffled. "Yeah. It wouldn't make me cry like right now when I saw it. I'd smile at it. And sometimes, like you said, we could look at it and smile together. Right?"

"Right," Mark said, his voice raspy with emotion.

Joey nodded slowly. "'Kay."

"Pick the one you want from the boxes at the bottom of the display," Mark said.

Joey scrutinized the selection of globes, picked one with skaters, then wrapped his arms around the box tightly, hugging it to his chest. "Can we go home now?" he said. "I gotta find a special place for this in my room."

"Sure," Mark said. "We'll finish up another time."

"Good." Joey nodded. "'Cause I really, really need to go home."

As they headed toward the cashier, Mark stopped by the tree with the baby ornaments and looked at Cedar. "Was there something here that *you* wanted?" he asked, looking at her intently. "You examined every one of these ornaments, Cedar. I was watching you do it. I'd like to buy you your favorite one since it's obvious they mean something special to you."

"Oh. No," she said, picking an imaginary thread from her sweater. "I just thought they were very cute, that's all. Thank you for the lovely offer, but…no, I don't want…what I mean is…come on, Joey, let's get in line at the cashier's booth. This is a busy place tonight, so we'd best get our spot so we don't have to stand there for a week."

"'Kay," Joey said, still clutching his precious purchase to his chest.

"Would you like the globe in a separate bag so you can carry it yourself?" Cedar asked.

"No, I don't think so," Joey said. "What if I drop it or something? Uncle Mark, will you carry it for me? But you gotta be super careful, you know?"

"You'd trust me with it?" Mark said, his heart doing a funny little two-step.

"Yeah," Joey said. "I trust you, Uncle Mark."

"Thank you," Mark said, then cleared his throat, "for that trust, Joey."

As they stood in the lengthy line, Mark stared at Cedar and narrowed his eyes. What was it going to take for Cedar to trust him as Joey did? She'd fumbled over her response to his offer to buy her a baby ornament, not meeting his gaze and sounding as phony as a three-dollar bill…if a three-dollar bill could talk. Damn it, was she pregnant with his baby? If she was, didn't she intend to tell him, for God's sake?

Well, he had news for Dr. Cedar Kennedy. At the first opportunity that arose he was going to confront her and get to the bottom of what was really going on. But, ah, damn, what was it going to take for Cedar to trust him the way Joey did?

The drive back to Mark's was made in total silence, with Cedar and Mark lost in their own thoughts and Joey nodding off to sleep. Joey woke when they arrived at the house and insisted on finding the right place to put the globe in his room before he went to bed.

"Aren't you coming, Cedar?" Joey asked, stopping as he and Mark started down the hallway toward his bedroom.

"I thought it best to wait for an invitation to go into your room, Joey," she said.

"Oh. Well, I invite you."

"Thank you," she said, smiling as she joined them in the hall.

The globe was put in the chosen spot, Joey got into his pajamas, and they both kissed him good night. Mark tipped the globe upside down and they all watched the fluffy snow cascade over the skaters.

Joey's eyes drifted closed and he was asleep before they quietly left the room.

"Something to drink?" Mark asked, when he and Cedar were once again in the living room.

"A soda would hit the spot," Cedar said.

"Want to add a bowl of ice cream to that?"

"No, I'm still full from all the pizza I indulged in. I'll sit with you while you have ice cream, though."

Mark nodded and they went into the kitchen. When they were finally seated across from each other at the table, Mark took a bite of his ice cream, then looked at Cedar. "Is there something you need to tell me?" he said.

"About the outing this evening?" Cedar said. "Well, the way Joey opened up about the snow globe was excellent. He trusts you now, Mark, and you should feel very good about that. You're doing a wonderful job with him."

"Thanks." Mark consumed another spoonful of ice cream. "I appreciate what you just said, but I was referring to *you,* personally, needing to tell me something."

Cedar frowned in confusion. "You've totally lost me."

"Come on, Cedar." Mark pushed the bowl aside and folded his arms on top of the table. "This is me, Mark, not some guy you just met a few hours ago. There was a lot more going on with you when you were looking at those baby ornaments than thinking they were cute. You're patting me on the head because Joey has come to trust me, but what I'm wondering is why *you* don't. Cedar, talk to me. What was going on with you and those baby ornaments?"

"Nothing. I—"

"I'm not buying that," Mark interrupted. He reached over and grasped one of her hands. "Cedar, are you pregnant with my baby, our baby?"

The color drained from Cedar's face and her voice was trembling when she spoke again. "And if I am?" she asked. "What then, Mark? How would you feel about that, about me carrying your child?" She pulled her hand free and crossed her arms beneath her breasts.

"How would I feel?" he said. "Oh, about one hundred feet tall. Thrilled out of my mind, that's how I'd feel. Ah, Cedar, don't you get it? I've fallen head over heels in love with you. I want to marry you, spend the rest of my life with you. We'd be a family, you, me, Joey, the baby I sure as hell hope you're pregnant with right now. I swear to heaven, Cedar Kennedy, that I love you."

Tears misted Cedar's eyes and she attempted to

blink them away. "You love me?" she asked. "And you hope I'm pregnant with your baby? That's quite an announcement, Mark. I guess you'd be strutting your machismo stuff to think you got me pregnant despite our using protection when we made love. You'd want to watch me grow big with your baby, show me off to all your buddies as evidence of your virility. That's what men want, isn't it? To produce an heir, an extension of themselves, their very own biological child that will announce to the world that you were here on this earth. Right?"

"What are you so angry about?" he said, throwing up his hands. "What did I do wrong here? I mean, cripe, I declare my love for you, tell you that if you're pregnant, it would be really fantastic, and you're mad as hell. Can I have a clue as to what is going on in that complicated mind of yours?"

Cedar sighed, a sad, weary-sounding sigh. "I'm not pregnant, Mark," she said softly, staring at the tabletop.

"Oh. Well, okay," he said with a shrug. "But you want to be, right? That's why you got all dewy looking at the baby ornaments." He paused. "Cedar, do you love me as much as I love you? Do you?"

"Yes," she whispered, "but—"

"All right!" he said, punching one fist in the air.

"This is dynamite. We'll get married and you can move in here instead of buying a different house. We'll be a family, you, me, Joey and we'll get started on creating that new baby. Oh, yeah, and we'll get Oreo a red sweater and—"

"Stop it," Cedar said, getting to her feet as tears slid down her cheeks. "I'm not going to marry you, Mark. Yes, I love you. I love Joey, too, but…no, you and I are not getting married. I'm not going to live here in this house, because I plan to buy a new place for me…for me and my…for me and my daughter."

"What daughter?" Mark said, rising. "You just said that you're not pregnant."

"I'm not," Cedar said, dashing the tears from her cheeks. "I'm adopting a baby girl when she's born in a couple of months. I didn't plan to tell anyone for fear the birth mother will change her mind at the last minute. But it's so hard not to daydream about that child being mine and…that's why I was looking at those ornaments the way that I was. I was imagining what it would be like next Christmas when Faith…I intend to name her Faith. I know I shouldn't have given her a name yet, but I couldn't help it. I want her to be mine so very much and…" She shook her head as a sob caught in her throat.

Mark walked around the table and drew Cedar into his embrace. "Look at me," he said.

Cedar shook her head.

"Look…at…me."

She raised her head slowly to meet his gaze, tears still glistening in her blue eyes.

"I won't pretend I'm not a bit stunned that you're planning to adopt a baby," he said, "but it sure says a lot. It tells me you're not as career-oriented as I thought, with no room for anything other than your work. That's great, Cedar.

"But are you refusing to marry me because you think I won't accept your daughter as my own child, give her my name, be her daddy? If that's where your mind went, then tell it to get back here because you're wrong. If she's *your* daughter, then she's *my* daughter, too. Just the way Joey would be *our* son. You're not giving me enough credit here."

"But…"

"Faith. That's nice. I like that name," he said, smiling at her. "Oh, man, this house will be filled with love and laughter and the sound of happy kids and…marry me, Cedar. Please. We'll be a family. A boy, a girl, then later…"

Cedar stepped back, breaking the embrace, and wrapped her hands around her elbows.

"Later what, Mark?" she whispered, her voice trembling. "We'll have child number three? The one we create together?"

"Well, sure, yeah."

"And if there isn't a third baby? What then?"

"Hey," Mark said, raising both hands. "Let's slow down a tad. We're getting way ahead of ourselves. You're focusing on becoming a mother of a newborn. I can understand why you would feel overwhelmed discussing another kiddo after that. Put that subject on the back burner. Why don't we talk about getting married?"

"No."

"No getting married talk yet. Right." Mark frowned. "Could you give me a hint as to what is a safe subject to address?"

"I…I think it would be best," Cedar said, lifting her chin, "if we just zero in on getting Joey through this first Christmas without his parents. He's doing so well, but it's far too early in his healing process to get complacent. Yes, that's what we should do. Concentrate on Joey."

Mark nodded slowly. "Okay. Then after the holidays we circle back around to us, you and me, our future together and—"

"Just stay in the present, Mark. Focus on Joey."

"Got it. Stay cool." He smiled. "Am I allowed to tell you that I love you? And could you toss out an I-love-you-too-Mark every once in a while?"

"Well, I…well, not when Joey can hear those

words spoken. He has enough to deal with right now."

"You're the shrinky-dink," Mark said, "but personally I believe that kid would be thrilled out of his socks if we were to get married and he was to get a baby sister and Oreo the cat."

"No, he's on emotional overload right now. Look how he fell apart when he saw the snow globe. The holidays are going to be very difficult for him and—"

"I get the picture," Mark interrupted. "There's a whole helluva lot of stuff being put on the back burner." He sighed. "All right, Cedar, we'll do this your way."

"Thank you," she said softly.

"But as soon as we see Joey safely through the holidays, then—"

"We'll…talk." Cedar managed to produce a small smile. "Your ice cream is turning soupy."

"Oh. Well, it tastes just as good that way, so I'll polish it off." Mark settled back into his chair at the table. "Care to join me?"

Cedar nodded and slid into her chair again.

"I love you," Mark said, looking at her. "You love me. Life is good. I'm a happy man." He shifted his attention to his bowl of melting ice cream.

Right now, Mark was a happy man, Cedar thought miserably. And right now she was, without a doubt, the most selfish woman on the face of the earth.

Mark believed that everything would fall into place for them after the holidays. But that wasn't true. Yes, she loved him. Oh, dear God, how she loved him. And to know that he loved her? It was beyond her wildest imagination.

But once the holidays were over and the new year had arrived, she wouldn't be accepting Mark's proposal. They wouldn't be telling Joey that he was getting a family that included her, Faith and Oreo the cat. They wouldn't be buying Oreo a red sweater.

No.

She couldn't marry Mark Chandler.

Not now.

Not later.

Not ever.

Chapter Thirteen

On Friday morning a week later, Cedar entered the office to find Bethany already typing on her computer keyboard.

"I'm early," Cedar said, smiling, "so that means you're *very* early. It's only a few weeks until Christmas. Are you trying to impress Santa Claus?"

"I'm just attempting to bring all these files up to date," Bethany said. "You have been extremely busy, Dr. Kennedy."

Cedar sighed. "I know, but it's so typical for this time of year. The majority of extra appointments have been with foster kids who have been removed from their own families. I've seen most of them outside the office, in festive settings, so they have to confront feelings brought on by the holidays."

"Is that what you're doing with Joey? And Uncle Mark?" Bethany wiggled her eyebrows. "Joey hasn't been in here in two weeks."

"Well, yes, the best way to ease Joey through the holidays has been to decorate a Christmas tree, buy gifts, wrap them, then stand by ready to soothe and comfort him if he has a bad moment when remembering doing those things with his parents."

"And how is he doing?"

"Joey is progressing well," Cedar said. "You'll see my notes when you get to his file. There have been a few tearful episodes about holiday details, but Mark has really bonded with him and Joey is willing to discuss how he feels. He trusts his Uncle Mark now."

"Do you?"

"Do I what?" Cedar asked.

"Trust Mark Chandler," Bethany said. "Come on, Cedar, give me a hint as to what is going on between you and Mark. I figured out he sent the flowers, remember? You're spending just as much time with him as you are with Joey. Oh, that Joey is a heartstealer, isn't he? Then again, maybe so is his Uncle Mark? Yes?"

As Cedar mentally scrambled for a reply, the telephone rang.

"I adore telephones," Cedar said, then made her escape into her office as Bethany lifted the receiver.

Cedar sank into the chair behind her desk and looked at the list of appointments she had that day that Bethany had placed squarely in the center of her desk. She leaned back and gently massaged her aching temples.

She was exhausted and the day had hardly begun. Yes, this was always a hectic time of year due to the needs of her young clients. But this year there was even more going on that was keeping her from getting the sleep she needed when she collapsed into bed each night.

She was living a charade, she thought, which was just a polite word for a lie. She could tell from the way Mark was acting that he believed they would be settling on a wedding date when they had their ever-famous *talk* after the holidays. He laughed easily, his smiles were genuine and there was such love shining in his eyes when he looked at her…and when they made love.

She'd lost count of how many times she'd become overwhelmed with guilt and started to tell Mark the truth, that she would not be accepting his proposal of marriage. But then she'd hesitate and the moment would be lost. She didn't want to ruin Mark's and Joey's Christmas. Or her own, to be truthful. She wanted—needed—the memories because that was all she would have so very, very soon.

"Well, well," Bethany mused, entering Cedar's office after knocking, "that was an interesting telephone conversation."

"Oh?" Cedar said, relieved to be pulled from her tormented thoughts.

"Yes, indeed," Bethany said, settling into one of the chairs in front of Cedar's desk. "It was our baby-having-a-baby Cindy calling. She was in a rush and was talking a hundred miles an hour. She just wanted me to give you a message."

Cindy changed her mind about the baby, Cedar thought, stiffening in her chair and feeling the color drain from her face. Oh, dear God, no.

"What…what did…she say?" she said, hearing the trembling in her voice.

Bethany beamed. "She said that she was so excited that you had agreed to adopt her baby girl that she forgot to double-check the one thing she wanted you to promise her. She said not to forget the bunny wallpaper."

"Oh," Cedar took a needed breath and placed a hand over her racing heart. "Thank God. I thought maybe… yes, of course, bunny wallpaper."

"I should be upset that you didn't tell me you were adopting Cindy's baby," Bethany said, "but I'm so thrilled for you that I won't pout. Oh, Cedar, you're going to be a mommy. This is fantastic. You can bring the baby to the office when she's small. I'll be in heaven. But why didn't you tell me you had this in motion? What does Mark think about you suddenly being a package deal, with more in that bundle than just Oreo?"

"Bethany, stop," Cedar said. "In the first place, I didn't tell you about the baby because I don't want to jinx things. I haven't even told my own parents. I still can't shake the fear that Cindy will change her mind."

"That's understandable," Bethany said, nodding, "but I don't think there's any chance of that now that I've spoken to her on the phone. She told me she's going to learn to surf when she moves to California with her family after the baby is born. That little girl is already looking to the future and it doesn't include having a baby in tow."

"I hope you're right." Cedar paused. "As for Mark, my decision has nothing to do with him. Faith will be *my* baby, *my* daughter. I'll be one of the multitude of single women balancing a career and motherhood. My family will be made up of me, Faith and Oreo."

"Faith. That's a pretty name. Does Mark like it?"

"Bethany, aren't you listening to me at all?" Cedar said, her voice rising. "Mark is not in the picture."

"Oh, baloney," Bethany said, getting to her feet. "I've seen the soft smiles when you say Mark's name, the flush on your cheeks, heard the way you talk about Joey." She frowned. "Honey, what are you afraid of? Why are you denying your feelings for Mark?"

Cedar picked up the list of appointments for the day. "I don't wish to discuss this further, Bethany," she said. "Please."

"All right, but I'm here if you want to talk." Bethany started toward the door. "I'm going out on my lunch break to buy some yarn so I can knit a sweater for Faith. Oh, that is a lovely name. I can hardly wait to get my hands on that wee one."

The telephone rang and Bethany hurried to her desk to answer the call. A moment later, she buzzed Cedar on the intercom to say that a man named Moose wished to speak with her.

"Hello, Moose," Cedar said, seconds later. "Merry Christmas."

"Same to you, Cedar," Moose said. "It's only two weeks away, by golly." He paused. "Did you get your copy of the appraisal of your house?"

"Yes, I did."

"Good. Hey, listen, I need to run this by you," he said. "I'm itching to get started on that gem of a house and so are my buddies, but my wife said I'm going to go Christmas shopping with her for the kids this year and help wrap the presents and peel potatoes for the big meal and—you get the drift. She said not even to think about that house until after the new year or she'd pop me one."

Cedar narrowed her eyes. "Oh, really? Your *wife* told you to postpone things? Mark had nothing to do with this revised schedule that puts our business on hold until the new year?"

"Mark who?" Moose said.

"Mmm," Cedar said. "Very interesting. If I could see you right now, Moose, I have a feeling I would be witnessing your nose growing."

"I knew I couldn't pull this off," Moose said, with a groan. "I'd make a lousy spy. I crumble under female pressure. Don't tell Mark I blew it, okay? He told me it was very important that you stay put and not contract for a new house until the holidays are over. Besides, I already told you there was no rush so this whole conversation is nuts. I'm sorry, Cedar."

Cedar sighed. "That's okay, Moose. I've been so busy, I haven't had a moment to even think about house shopping. As far as Mark pulling strings and pushing buttons...well, I'll address that issue with him."

"Oh, man, that boy is in trouble. Then I'll be in deeper trouble because he'll know I messed up and...this is bad, very bad."

"I'll make clear that I figured it out on my own, Moose," Cedar said. "Have a wonderful Christmas and we'll think about the house in a few weeks."

"Thanks, Cedar. See ya."

"See ya," she said, then replaced the receiver slowly.

Mark Chandler, she thought, you are rotten to the core. He was making certain that she would be free to move from her falling-down house into his super-duper house without the hassle of breaking a contract for a new place. Really sneaky.

And what are you? she asked herself in the next instant. She was living a lie every time she was with Mark. Talk about rotten. She didn't have the right to confront Mark about his scheme. Moose was off the hook, the big softy. Oh, well.

"Cheer up, Cedar," she ordered herself aloud. "Think happy thoughts. Think about...yes, think about bunny wallpaper."

The following Saturday night, after yet another busy week, Cedar joined Mark and Joey for a live performance of the *Nutcracker.* Mark looked handsome in his dark-blue suit with a pale-blue shirt and dark-blue tie. Joey looked adorable in his gray slacks and holiday sweater with a reindeer prancing across his little chest. Joey was totally captivated by the show, but Cedar noticed that Mark kept shifting in his seat and looking at his watch.

"Sit still," Cedar finally whispered. "What is your problem?"

"I hate ballets," Mark muttered, his voice hushed. "Every time the story gets rolling, they stop and dance forever. It drives me up the wall."

Cedar laughed. "Well, Joey is enthralled, so grit your teeth and suffer through this."

"I'm having a banana split when we go for ice cream after this thing," Mark said. "The bigger the better because I've earned it."

"Shh," a woman in front of them hissed, turning to glare.

"Sorry," Cedar said.

"I don't want to be here," Mark said, close to Cedar's ear.

"Don't pout. You can't always have your own way, you know."

"But some things are so important that I'll do whatever I possibly can to accomplish what I've set out to do." Mark looked into her eyes. "Like convincing you to marry me."

"Like conning Moose into calling me with his phony story?" she said, raising her eyebrows.

"He told me you nailed him." Mark chuckled. "Well, you win some and lose some along the way. The thing that matters is the final outcome. Why don't you put me out of my misery and accept my proposal now, instead of making me wait until after the holidays are over? Come on, Cedar. Say yes."

"Shh," the woman in front of them hissed once more.

"Thank you, ma'am," Cedar said, then redirected her attention to the characters on the stage.

"Hell," Mark muttered, then looked at his watch again.

The stress of waiting for the big discussion with Cedar was getting to him, he admitted to himself. Christmas was only a week away. It would be sensational to be able to tell Joey on Christmas morning that Cedar was to become a part of their family, that she was adopting a baby sister for Joey and that Oreo would be moving into the house, too.

Mark shifted in the chair again, then looked at his watch again.

Why did Cedar get to call all the shots? he thought as he appraised the woman beside him in the mauve suit and pale-pink silk blouse. The man-and-woman part of their lives was just as important as the father-and-mother part. Surely Cedar could see that Joey was coming along great and there was no need for them to postpone making plans for a future that included all of them…together.

The heck with this schedule Cedar had put in place. They were going to have a serious discussion *tonight* after they got Joey tucked into bed. Yes, sir, by damn, tonight was the night.

Mark jerked in his seat as the audience erupted in cheers and applause.

"The performance is over, Mark, and you lived to tell about it," Cedar said, as they got to their feet.

"It was way cool," Joey said. "Didn't you like it, Uncle Mark?"

"It wasn't exactly my thing," Mark said, pulling the knot of his tie down several inches, "but I'm glad you enjoyed it, Joey. I'm ready for some ice cream. Yep, we'll stop for a snack, then get you home and into bed, buddy. You must be tired because it's already past your bedtime."

"I'm not tired," Joey said.

"Sure you are," Mark said. "Let's hustle over to the ice cream place, then go straight home."

Just over an hour later, Cedar and Mark tucked Joey into bed, kissed him good-night, then Mark turned the globe upside down to produce the fluffy snow that floated over the skaters.

"Sleep well, Joey," Cedar said.

"Yeah," Joey mumbled, then yawned. "You, too."

Mark chuckled. "Down for the count."

When they'd returned to the living room, Cedar declined Mark's offer of something to drink after settling onto the sofa. Mark remained standing.

"All right," she said, crossing her legs and tapping her foot. "Are you ready to tell me what's going on? You've been acting weird all evening. And don't try to tell me it's because you don't like ballets."

Mark sank into an easy chair and cleared his throat, then cleared it again. "Okay, here goes," he said finally. "Cedar, wouldn't you agree that Joey is doing extremely well, except, of course, for the few times that he got upset about his parents, which is understandable because after all it hasn't been that long since they—anyway, he's doing good, right?"

"Yes, he is," Cedar acknowledged, nodding. "Much better, in fact, than I expected under the circumstances. I'm very pleased."

"Dandy. Now, due to Joey's fine emotional progress I believe that adjustments should be made in the scheduling of things."

"What things?" Cedar asked, frowning.

"Things like...like us," Mark said. "There's no

reason why we can't discuss our future together, Cedar. It isn't necessary to wait until the holidays are over. Think how great it would be to tell Joey on Christmas that you and I are getting married, that you're moving in here with Oreo and that a few weeks after that he'll have a new baby sister named Faith."

"Oh, but…" Cedar started, feeling the color drain from her face.

"Hear me out." Mark raised one hand. "I love you, Cedar, and you love me. There's nothing standing in our way of becoming a family. We could include Joey in the whole deal, too, take him along when we pick out our wedding rings, let him help us get the nursery ready for Faith and—"

"No," Cedar snapped, getting to her feet. "Stop it, Mark. Don't push me like this. We agreed to wait, to have a lovely Christmas with Joey and…you're going to ruin everything by insisting we address all this now. Just stop it."

"Why?" He got to his feet and crossed the room to stand a few feet away from her. "I don't understand. Damn it, Cedar, there's something you're not telling me and I want to know what it is."

"I'll tell you after the holidays," she said, her voice rising. "That's when we agreed to discuss all this."

"There's no reason to wait," Mark said, matching

her volume. "Are you, or are you not going to be my wife, Cedar?"

"No!"

"Why the hell not?" Mark yelled.

Tears filled Cedar's eyes as she opened her mouth to reply. Before she could speak she gasped as she saw Joey enter the room. He was dragging Puncho the clown toward them.

When Joey reached them, he set Puncho squarely between them, looked at Mark, then Cedar, then back at Mark, a stricken expression on his face. Without saying a word, he turned and went back down the hallway.

"Oh, God," Cedar whispered, as tears spilled onto her cheeks. "Joey told Puncho his innermost secrets, his feelings, and he felt so much better for having done it. He thinks Puncho can solve our problems, too. That's why he brought his clown to us. Did you see the expression on Joey's face? He's devastated because we're shouting at each other."

"Yeah, I know," Mark said, dragging a restless hand through his hair. "I feel like the scum of the earth for upsetting him. Great father I am." He sighed. "I suppose I should say we'll go back to your schedule for discussing our future, but I can't do that, Cedar. Not after you've said…yelled…that you have no intention of marrying me. I need to know why you won't become my wife."

Mark glanced toward the hallway, looked at Puncho, then took Cedar's hand. "Let's sit down and talk…quietly," he said. "This can't be postponed any longer."

Struggling against her tears, Cedar settled onto the sofa with Mark, both of them shifting slightly to face each other.

"Why?" Mark said, looking into Cedar's eyes.

Cedar drew a shuddering breath before she attempted to speak.

"You know that I was married," she said, meeting Mark's gaze. "Gary and I were high-school sweethearts and we got married right after we graduated. I worked as a secretary in a bank and he was a mechanic. We were blissfully happy even though we lived in a dinky little apartment and lived paycheck to paycheck. Then I got pregnant and even though we couldn't afford a baby at that time, we were thrilled. When I was five months along, I had a miscarriage."

"Oh, man, that's rough," Mark said, frowning.

"It was a very…violent…miscarriage and I was hemorrhaging out of control. The baby was gone and the only way to save *my* life was for the doctors to perform a hysterectomy. I was nineteen years old and told I would never have children.

"It was a very stressful and sad time and Gary struggled with the fact that I would never have his baby. Months later, he told me that he just couldn't deal with it, knowing he would never be the father of his own child, that he couldn't accept the concept of adopting someone else's baby. He…he said he wanted a divorce."

Mark muttered an earthy expletive and took Cedar's hands in his.

"I ran home to my parents for comfort and hardly functioned for months," Cedar continued. "Then I decided I had to get on with my life, having made a very major decision. I would never love again. Never. My inability to have children would eventually destroy any relationship I might enter into, and I was determined to protect myself from that pain.

"I got my degree in child psychology so I could direct my maternal instincts toward troubled kids to teach them how to be happy, how to smile again. Those kids would fill the empty place in my heart that longed for a family of my own."

"Ah, Cedar," Mark said, shaking his head.

"Everything went as planned until…until I met you, Mark. You and Joey. I didn't mean to fall in love with you. I was furious with myself that I had lost control of my emotions. I should have told you the truth early on and ended things, but I was so happy with you, cherishing all the memories I was collecting like precious gems, and...I was selfish to do what I did and I'm sorry, so very sorry.

"Now you understand why I can't marry you. You've already spoken of the child we'll create together when Faith gets older." Tears spilled onto Cedar's cheeks. "But that isn't going to happen, Mark. I can't give you a child and that truth will chip away at what we have together until there's nothing left." She pulled her hands free and dashed the tears from her face. "I'm sorry I led you on, didn't tell you sooner. Maybe we can pretend everything is all right so Joey can have a nice Christmas, then I'll disappear from your life the way I should have weeks ago."

"No," Mark said.

"Oh, Mark, I know you're angry at my deception, but can't we think about Joey? About how he needs this Christmas as part of his healing process?"

"No. I mean...no, you're misunderstanding me, Cedar." Mark got to his feet. "Let me show you something."

Mark crossed the room to the Christmas tree and retrieved a present. Cedar got to her feet and met him halfway as he was returning to her, Puncho standing beside them.

"Open this," Mark said, handing her the small gift.

"What is it?"

"You'll see," he said.

Cedar hesitated, then removed the bright paper, dropping it to the floor.

"What…" she said, frowning.

"That's a red sweater for Oreo," Mark said, "and those red booties are for Faith because I couldn't find a bright red baby sweater. They're for our family photo op. *Our family.* We'll have a son named Joey. A daughter named Faith. A cat named Oreo. And we'll add a dog at some point to round out the pet part.

"Ah, Cedar, don't you see how blessed we are already? A boy and a girl. A son, a daughter. What more could we ask for? On top of that, we love each other, by damn, and it just doesn't get any better than that."

"But you said we'd create a child together and—"

"I know I said that." Mark smiled. "And I lost sleep over it, too, because you're dealing with the original worry machine when it comes to providing for my family the way I want to. *Three* kids? How was I going to put braces on three sets of teeth, feed and clothe three, put three through college?

"But I figured I'd have to sweat it in silence because you deserved the right to have a baby and I couldn't deprive you of that. I knew in my heart that Joey and Faith were all I needed as a father, but I resigned myself to getting ulcers, stewing about providing for all of us while keeping my mouth shut about it."

"Mark?" Cedar sniffed, clutching the sweater and booties to her heart. "Are you really saying that…? I can't believe this."

"Cedar, I'm so sorry you had a rough time way back when. It must have been hell. But you have just taken a load off my back that was weighing me down something fierce."

"But what if you change your mind?" Cedar asked, "realize we could afford three children and—"

"Then we'll adopt another one." Mark threw up his arms. "But don't count on that happening because I'll probably take five years deciding if we can budget in the dog." He framed her face in his hands. "Ah, Cedar, we have it all *right now*. A never-ending love for each other, a super son and a precious daughter on the way. Oh, and your weird fat cat. Marry me. Be my wife, my life's partner, the mother of our children, Joey and Faith. Please?"

"Oh, dear heaven." Fresh tears filled Cedar's eyes. "Yes, I'll marry you. Thank you for being you, for being a money worrywart and…oh, God, I love you so much."

With Oreo's sweater and Faith's booties held in one hand, Cedar flung her arms around Mark's neck as he wrapped his arms around her to pull her close. He captured her mouth in a searing kiss that sealed their commitment to all the tomorrows they would share as a family.

"Hooray," Joey yelled, running into the room.

Cedar and Mark jerked apart, then Mark scooped up Joey into his arms.

"Hey, Joey, thanks for the use of your Puncho," Mark said. "You're a smart guy. So, how about it? Shall we be a family? I'll be the dad, Cedar the mom, you're the son and you'll have a baby sister named Faith and a cat named Oreo."

"And a dog?" Joey said.

"Don't push your luck," Mark said. "Well, how does the family photo op I just described sound to you, buddy?"

"Cool," Joey yelled, punching one fist in the air. "Way cool."

Mark smiled and extended his other arm toward Cedar, who stepped into his embrace eagerly, nestling her head on his chest as she splayed a hand on Joey's back.

"Way, way cool," she said, tears of joy in her eyes.

No one noticed that the smile on Puncho the clown's face suddenly seemed to grow bigger and brighter.

Ten Months Later

"Okay, folks, I know you're warm under those lights, so let's get going," the photographer said.

"You look real spiffy in your red sweaters…all of you, including the cat and the dog. Yep, this will make a dandy Christmas card. You want all your names printed below the picture, right? Cedar and Mark, Joey and Faith, Oreo and Pretzel. Got it. Ready? Then smile, Chandler family. That's it. Perfect. You're absolutely perfect."

* * * * *

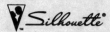

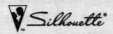

SPECIAL EDITION™

Don't miss the latest book from

Sharon De Vita

coming in October 2005!

ABOUT THE BOY

Silhouette Special Edition #1715

When widow Katie Murphy moved back
to Cooper's Cove to run the newspaper,
she sought a role model for her sun, Rusty.
Police chief Lucas Porter proved to be the
perfect mentor—but relations between
Katie and Lucas weren't smooth. Could the
redheaded reporter overcome Lucas's
distrust of the media…and earn
a press pass to his heart?

Available at your favorite retail outlet.

Where love comes alive™

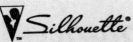

COMING NEXT MONTH

SSECNM0905